The Secret Husband, The O'Connells
Paperback Copyright © 2023 Lorhainne Ekelund
Editor: Talia Leduc

ISBN-13: 978-1-989698-42-6

Give feedback on the book at:
lorhainneeckhart@hotmail.com

Twitter: @LEckhart
Facebook: AuthorLorhainneEckhart

Printed in the U.S.A

The Secret Husband

THE O'CONNELLS
BOOK THREE

LORHAINNE ECKHART

"This is another one of Lorhainne's inimitable, intense reads that sucked me in right from the beginning...A gritty, emotionally gripping story with quite a few surprises and twists that I really loved reading."

HONEST BOOKWORM

"This is a real intriguing tale, filled with unexpected and surprising twists. Karen's secret past comes back in the most unusual way when her ex-husband calls for help...it sure kept me reading from beginning to end. An engaging addition to this wonderful series!"

CATLOU

"This is a story where the lines of the right and wrong, or the black and white of life is blurry. A reminder that life is messy and the future is an unknown...Another thought provoking story by this talented author."

Y. CRUZ, REVIEWER

About the O'Connells

The O'Connells of Livingston, Montana, are not your typical family. Follow them on their journey to the dark and dangerous side of love in a series of romantic thrillers you won't want to miss. Raised by a single mother after their father's mysterious disappearance eighteen years ago, the six grown siblings live in a small town with all kinds of hidden secrets, lies, and deception. Much like the contemporary family romance series focusing on the Friessens, this romantic suspense series follows the lives of the O'Connell family as each of the siblings searches for love.

The O'Connells

The Neighbor
The Third Call
The Secret Husband
The Quiet Day
The Commitment, An O'Connell Novella
The Missing Father
The Hometown Hero

Justice
The Family Secret
The Fallen O'Connell
The Return of the O'Connells
And The She Was Gone
The Stalker
The O'Connell Family Christmas
The Girl Next Door
Broken Promises
The Gatekeeper
The Hunted

The O'Connells Box Set Collections

The O'Connells Books 1 - 3
The O'Connells Books 4 - 6
The O'Connells Books 7 - 9
The O'Connells Books 10 - 12
The O'Connells Books 13 - 15

A shocking phone call. An ex-husband in deep trouble. Will a lawyer's decision to help him take a dark turn she'll regret?

Small-town lawyer Karen O'Connell believes that all of her clients who have found themselves recklessly embroiled in scandal and trouble have done so foolishly because of love. She has heard far too many times that the heart wants what it wants.

But one night, Karen receives a call from Jack Curtis, her vengeful ex-husband, whom she's never told anyone in her family about. He's found himself in a world of trouble, arrested and in jail, charged with murder.

He says he's innocent, and he needs her help.

Her first response is to say no, but Karen knows Jack isn't the kind of guy to ask for help from anyone, especially not from the ex-wife he openly despises and hasn't seen in years. She knows there must be more to the story—but what she doesn't know is that the mysterious circumstances surrounding the murder could be the reason their hasty marriage ended so badly.

CHAPTER

One

ALTHOUGH SOME COUPLES bragged of Friday date nights filled with romance and dinner, followed by extremely hot sex, Karen O'Connell's Friday nights unfortunately consisted of a quiet, darkened office, a shot of whiskey, and the locked drawer in her desk that only she ever went into.

She stared at the names on the files that filled the drawer, names that were meaningless to the masses but left her reaching for the bottle of whiskey she kept tucked in the back, a single short lead-cut crystal highball glass, and a green velvet ring box. The drawer was a constant reminder, like an albatross around her neck, of everything wrong with her life.

She only opened it on Friday nights or when she needed to add yet another file, a case where she hadn't secured the win her client deserved. It was a drawer that, she supposed, if she had to put a label on it, symbolized sorrow, heartache, pain, grief, anger, every sickening emotion that seemed to encompass what the legal system was becoming more and more as of late.

These were the kinds of defeats and sorrows she didn't share with anyone. How could she? Right and wrong seemed so unfair, leaving her filled with such anger, a trait in her that others considered unreasonable. At times, people compared her to a pit bull, not understanding what really drove her. But considering the names on these files all came with faces that haunted Karen every night when she closed her eyes, this was a fight she couldn't figure out how to win.

Why did she do this to herself? If she were like every other lawyer out there, she'd have told herself she'd done the best she could, that this was just the nature of her job, and to move on. But to Karen, these lost cases were lives that had been destroyed—mothers, daughters, fathers, brothers, husbands. They were each someone's child, and every one of them had been on the wrong side of the crap-shoot called justice. Being on the other side left Karen feeling so damn helpless.

She lifted the short glass and downed another swallow of the two fingers of whiskey, her secret indulgence, one no one in her family knew about. She kicked off her pumps, letting her bare toes dig into the carpet, and swiveled around and leaned back in her chair, taking in the two large windows that looked out at the darkened downtown.

Just then, the phone started ringing, and she did what she always did on Friday night: ignored it and let voicemail pick it up.

She waited until it stopped ringing before she settled into the vibration of the bass from the downstairs bar, welcoming the distraction. In that second of near silence, she lifted the glass and took another swallow, relishing the burn, and then let out a sigh. She turned back around, taking in the pile of files. Reine Colbert's, her most recent case, was on top. As she opened the file and read everything, the angst of it had her wishing she could have done more for a woman she felt had been screwed by everyone. She lifted the bottle, seeing it was half full, and poured another two fingers just as her cell phone lit up.

"Persistent, aren't they?" she said to no one as she took in the caller ID. It was Owen, her brother, who'd been more of a father to her—to all of their siblings, even though he'd been just a kid himself—than their own dad, whom she'd loved more than anything but who had decided to fuck off one day without even a goodbye to any of them.

Her hand hovered over the red decline, but at the same time, Owen was the one who never called. She answered. "Any chance that was you who called the office a second ago?"

"So you are there," he said. "Is that how you answer the phone?"

She didn't pick up her cell phone but left it on the desk, leaving the speaker on. Her brother's voice seemed to hold an edge. "It is when someone's phoning and bugging me when I just want to be left alone." She swirled the amber liquid as she made herself close up Reine's file. Under it was Lawrence Green's, another sad case, one of her first where the defendant ended up doing time for a crime she knew, deep down, he hadn't committed.

"I guess that answers my question as to where you are. Was at Marcus and Charlotte's new place, setting up Eva's bunk bed. We just picked it up. Everyone's there except you. Suzanne said you've got some standing appointment on Fridays, and Ryan said he'd heard that too, but then, as everyone was talking about you, which you know we all do, things didn't jive. I know you stay at the office every Friday night, but doing what? That, I haven't figured out yet."

She couldn't help the amusement that tugged at her

lips even though she felt like crap, considering Owen was a plumber, not a detective. "You spying on me?"

He said nothing for a second, and she wasn't sure what she heard in the background. "Don't need to. Generally, I just know what you're doing, what you're thinking, where you are, and when something is off with you. The fact that your office light is still on…"

She turned in her chair, feeling the hair on the back of her neck spike. "Uh…where are you?" She stood up, going to the window and looking out and down on the street, where her brother's plumbing van was parked out front.

Owen was standing there on the sidewalk, looking up and giving her a wave. "Let me in," he said. "Your door's locked." Then he hung up.

"Shit…" she said under her breath.

There was something about him tonight. On the phone, Owen hadn't sounded like himself. She wasn't in the mood to talk, but she rested the glass on the desk with the files and hurried barefoot to her office door. After pulling it open, she took in the empty desk of the receptionist she still needed to hire and strode to the stairs, down the dirty wood steps, which needed a sweep and a wash.

Her brother was looking at her through the commercial glass. She'd see what he wanted and send him on his way. Owen was dressed, as he always was, in blue jeans that had seen better days and a T-shirt, appearing as if he'd just been at a job site. She, meanwhile, was still in her navy dress.

She flicked the lock, and he pulled the door open and somehow maneuvered her back as he stepped in, flicking the deadbolt behind him. He was the same height and build as all her brothers, tall and broad shouldered, and he had the same O'Connell blue eyes, but at least he'd shaved.

"Drinking alone?" Ah, so he could smell it.

"And working…" she said as she crossed her arms, taking in the way he looked down at her before starting up the stairs ahead of her. "Where are you going?"

"Upstairs, to your office," he said, and she hurried after him, wanting to stuff the files back in the drawer along with the whiskey, which was sitting open on her desk.

"Hey, Owen, just give me a second to clean up," she said as she raced around him to her door, not having to turn around to know he was right behind her.

"You have a new client or case coming up?"

Once inside, she reached for the bottle and screwed the cap back on, not missing his expression, the way he took in her desk, the files, the bottle, everything.

"Wow, single malt, strong, bold. You can pour me a glass," he said, not waiting for her answer.

Her brain was still trying to come up with a story that sounded reasonable as she watched her brother make himself comfortable in the chair across from her desk, where every client who came to her for help sat. Owen, though, lifted his sneakered feet and rested them on her desk, crossing them. His gaze took in the files again, and she couldn't help feeling as if he were seeing into her secret, private self, which she showed no one.

She just held the bottle and took in the glass on her desk, then the washed empty mug that had held her coffee that morning. She poured a splash in the mug and took in his gesture for more.

"Bad day?" he added as she handed him the mug before sitting down in her chair and lifting her own glass.

She considered what to say, resting her hand on the files as Owen's gaze locked on to hers. Of course, he could see the names. She had a thing for big bold print on file tabs.

"Same as any other," she finally replied and settled her

glass back on the desk. She gathered the files and stuffed them back into the drawer along with the bottle of whiskey, then closed it and turned the key, which was still in the lock. She pulled it out and rested it on the desk, taking in the way her brother was watching her.

"You know you did the best you could," he said. "No one could have done more than you. Give yourself a break. So is this you punishing yourself? I don't get it."

She didn't say anything for a second, then took in the smile that really wasn't a smile on her brother's face as he lifted the mug and downed the rest of the liquor. The way he pulled in a breath, she knew he too relished the burn.

She went to say something, then decided against it, lifting her glass and swirling around the amber liquid. "So what are you doing here?"

Owen rested the mug on her scratched old desk and took his time looking around her office. "Truth? Checking on you, considering what happened to Reine Colbert. I knew you took it hard, and everyone was wondering about you and how you really are. This looks like a Friday-night pity party."

She froze, listening to the tick of the clock on the wall above the file cabinet, which held cases and clients and documents that didn't carry the same emotional baggage that her drawer of sorrow did. She flicked her eyes up and took in the intensity of her brother's gaze. Okay, so he knew, maybe?

"Ah…" was all she could get out. She sat back in her chair, hearing the woosh. "Pity party." She tried to conjure up something profound, but nothing came.

Owen just lifted his hand in a wave, the same motion he had used with all of them, growing up, when he wanted them to stop whatever bullshit was about to come out of their mouths. How in the hell had he ever managed to step into the role of their father? He'd been just a teenager, sixteen.

"You think I didn't figure it out some time ago?" he said. "This Friday night thing, this ritual you have…" He gestured to her desk, her glass. "Drinking whiskey and staying at the office—doing what, I wasn't really sure. I have to wonder, from those old case files on your desk, if that's part of it."

"What do you think you know? Seriously, Owen, every good lawyer looks at those lost cases because that's what makes you a better lawyer. You're being ridiculous. So what if I'm here, working?" Her bare feet hit the floor, and both her palms were flat on the desk.

Owen jabbed a finger to her glass. "You're drinking the hard stuff that you never drink."

"Who else knows?"

He raised a brow, always the silent observer. "Well, I had an idea. Pretty sure Luke does, too. I know Suzanne has wondered. Marcus and Ryan…" He just shrugged. "They're wrapped up in their stuff. Every Friday night you make some excuse, yet I see the lights on in your office, and I figured out the whiskey thing because Marcus mentioned he spotted you leaving the liquor store with it. Suzanne said she's seen you leaving the office late on Friday night a couple times when she's been out on a call, and you walk instead of drive. We all know when you've been drinking. Luke said we need to give you space while you figure out how to deal with a bad loss, because we know how person-ally you take your cases. You seem to forget I listen to everyone and put the puzzle together. Guess I just don't understand why you put yourself through it."

There it was. Her secret was unraveling. How could she explain to anyone when she didn't understand herself?

"Is it too much to ask for a little privacy in this family?"

she said, reaching for her glass and leaning back. She turned her chair to the side as she took another swallow.

"Karen, Karen, Karen, you should know better. Privacy in our family? You forget, I've been watching your back for how long? As for the whiskey thing, don't worry. No one in the family would believe you drink it. Marcus likely thought you were picking it up for someone. This pity party, you looking at those cases or whatever you're doing, no one else has figured it out."

"But you have." She turned to her brother, who ran his hand over his face.

He was handsome, a catch, yet he was as single as she, Luke, and Suzanne were. The one they all depended on, Owen was only a few years older, yet he had been a father to them all. Maybe the day their father left was the day she'd decided to hide everything she was thinking and feeling. Every man who'd ever said he loved her had turned his back on her and walked away, except her brothers.

"Yeah, always had my eye on you," Owen said. "The trouble you'd get into… Your prickly personality pushes everyone away, and at times you just can't help but make things difficult for yourself, with the way you'd scrap with Mom, with anyone and everyone. You need to let those cases go. You did more than anyone could do."

"They got a raw deal, Owen. You know, when I went to law school and then started practicing, I never realized law is just a different version of poker, a game of chance, where your life is in the hands of someone who doesn't know who you truly are. It's a toss of the dice, all up to whether the DA got laid the night before, or is fighting with his wife, or has profiled you because of the color of your skin, or because you're poor, or because you're a woman, or because you didn't come from a good home, a good neighborhood, or because you pissed off the wrong person, because, because… I could keep going. Racial and social profiling are things everyone does, but at the same time, you'll never get a judge, DA, or defense lawyer, never mind your average person out there, to admit they do it, because then they'd have to admit that this broken system doesn't work, and everyone's preconceived ideas about people and situations are in fact what should be on trial."

There she went, on a roll. She wasn't sure, by the way her brother cocked a brow, whether he was about to mock her, scold her, or tell her to get over herself.

Instead, he pulled in a breath. "Wow, you really are stuck in a dark place. I hope this isn't a place you go often, as it's not helping you or anyone and can make you bitter."

The way he said it felt so much like a scolding that she wanted to snarl.

He held up a hand. "You think I don't know all that? Of course I do. I saw the closed doors Mom faced, even though no one else did. But give yourself a break, Karen. It's the way the world works and always has. You're making a difference, and you need to start looking at what's working instead of what isn't. This dark place your head is in isn't doing you any good."

He gestured to her desk. "I know all those cases you've lost stick with you. If you had been any other lawyer, though, it would have been far worse for them. Reine Colbert would have gotten a lot more time, Lawrence Green would've been in a supermax in another state, where his family couldn't visit, Janine Baker wouldn't be up for parole next month, with a chance to reunite with her family, and Matt Wilky would never see the light of day again instead of having the chance of parole in fifteen years, all because he was in the wrong place at the wrong time.

"You want me to go on? Yeah, those cases sucked, and

I saw how you took what happened personally after each one. But no one could have done better. It was a crapshoot for them anyway. You think I don't know how you see a part of yourself in those cases that everyone else calls a lost cause? So how about you start telling yourself that you give a damn, and you did what you could, but it's not all on you?"

She just stared at her brother. "Is this a pep talk?" She settled her glass on the desk, crossing her legs again, leaning back. "Because, in case you didn't get the memo, I'm a big girl and can look after myself."

"If that's what you need to tell yourself, then so be it, but you're still my little sister, and a pain in the ass, too. You always did take things way too personally. You can't fix everything for everyone. Sometimes you're just going to have to tell yourself that you did all you could, and that's the best that can be hoped for. Life isn't always fair, Karen. It can suck sometimes, too."

She didn't know why, but the way Owen said it had her leaning forward on the desk, really looking at him. He never said anything about what was going on in his life. Instead, he was always steady for all of them.

"You okay there, Owen? You know, I'm getting the feeling something is going on with you. You know you don't always have to be the one who carries everything for everyone else. You know you can tell me—" The office phone rang. She stared at it, and so did her brother. Damn the interruption. Who the hell was calling now?

"You going to answer that?" he said.

Well, Owen showing up had ruined her melancholic Friday night alone time anyway. She hadn't even had the chance to settle into the files, which were back under lock and key. She let out a sigh and reached for the phone.

"So who is it?" Owen said. "Mom, Suzanne, Ryan, Marcus…?"

She pressed the phone to her ear. "Karen O'Connell. The office is now closed, so unless this is really—"

"Karen."

It was his voice. Deep, dark. It sucked her right back into that girl who had been nothing in his shadow. Her heart thudded, and she had to remind herself to breathe. She turned her chair, knowing her brother was watching her too closely.

"Are you there?" he said.

She breathed out the hurt, the ache, because she'd never expected to hear from him again, not after what he'd done to her.

"Yes, I'm here. Why are you calling?" She knew Owen was listening.

"So you know who this is?" the man said.

Of course she did. What was it about the voice of Jack Curtis, the first man she'd ever loved, the one she'd married, who'd broken her heart?

"You know what?" she said. "This really isn't a good time for me, so if you don't mind…" She went to turn around and hang up.

"Wait, don't hang up. I need your help. And you know I wouldn't call you unless the situation were really…dire."

In the window, Owen's reflection was watching in that way he did, listening to everything she was saying—and everything she wasn't.

She lowered her voice. "What I know is that I'm not supposed to be talking to you. You made sure of that with the last set of cops you sent. You've made your feelings for me very, very clear, so if you don't mind, I'm going to hang up now." She leaned forward and started to turn around again.

"Wait, Karen, don't hang up. Look, I'm sorry, but I'm in trouble—the kind of trouble that has me calling the last woman I would expect to help me."

"No, you look. I don't know what this is or what kind of trouble you're in, but let me remind you clearly of your words to me: You hate me, you want nothing to do with me, ever, and you never want to hear from me, talk to me, or see me again. In other words, I was and am very much dead to you, and—"

"I'm in jail," Jack said. "I've been charged with murder. I didn't do it."

She found herself staring at the phone for a second before putting it back to her ear.

"So if you could put everything aside, please," he said, "because I need your help."

She just lifted her gaze to the ceiling and leaned back in the chair. She couldn't face Owen, very aware of how her end of the conversation likely sounded to him.

"Hello, Karen, are you there?" he said. "Don't talk. Just listen. This is my one phone call. I'm in Sweetwater County Jail, and I'm stuck here until I go before a judge Monday morning. You know what that means."

"Why me?" She let out a sigh.

"Because there's something else you don't know," he said. She thought she heard someone in the background. "Look, my time is up. I've got to go. Please, Karen, just please, show up, help me."

The line went dead, and she pulled the phone from her ear before turning her chair around and setting the receiver back in the cradle. It took her another second before she could look over to her brother. Owen was too damn perceptive at times, which only added to Karen's unease.

"You want to tell me what that was about?" Owen

gestured to the phone and settled his feet back on the floor, not pulling his gaze from her. "Sounded to me like trouble. You in trouble? Something happen? Who aren't you supposed to contact? You know I can call Marcus…"

She found herself shaking her head. "It's someone I haven't heard from in years, something that ended badly. You know that one person you never want to hear from, and then they call? Well, he called because he's just landed in a shitload of trouble."

Owen didn't pull his gaze. "Sounded like more than that, Karen. You may as well just tell me, because I'll figure it out."

She took in her desk, the empty glass, and her brother, who didn't seem too interested in moving. "This stays between us, Owen. That was my husband," she said. "He's apparently in jail. I haven't talked to him in years. He hates me, and I very much hate him. Things ended very, very badly, and I never expected to hear from him again, especially after he called the cops on me and got a restraining order, but hey…" She gestured to the phone as if that explained everything. She could honestly say she'd never seen Owen appear so shocked. He didn't wear it well.

"Right, good, glad to have this talk." She tapped her desk, trying to settle herself. "Since you're struggling to find something to say, let me help you. I didn't tell anyone I got married. I hid it from all of you. It was a stupid-ass thing to do, but that was a time in my life when I was doing stupid-ass things. I've grown up now. Is there more to the story? Yes, absolutely. If you could just keep this little bombshell to yourself…"

Owen exhaled roughly and lifted his hand for her to stop talking. "What the hell, Karen? I think you'd better start at the beginning." He sounded unusually calm. "And this time, don't leave anything out."

CHAPTER
Two

KAREN TOOK in the gray concrete walls of a place where she'd spent way too much time with people who'd found themselves on the wrong side of the law. She struggled between being overwhelmed and numb now as she listened to the echoes from the hall outside, wondering too many things.

Had the deputy who'd led her to the interrogation room been able to smell the liquor on her? She should have gone home instead of the one place that was no good for her. She shouldn't be there now, and she didn't know what she was more freaked out over, the fact that she'd dropped her little bomb about Jack Curtis to her brother when she'd sworn to take it to her grave or the fact that she was now waiting for the man she loved and hated all because he'd called her for help. Like, who did that? Evidently, she still hadn't learned.

The clang of the heavy metal door had her heartbeat kicking up again. She couldn't sit; instead, she stood against the concrete wall, feeling dampness under her arms that she knew her silky cap-sleeved dress wouldn't hide.

Her toes ached from the four-inch pumps she'd shoved her swollen feet back into as she waited for a man she hadn't seen in eight years.

Jack Curtis was cuffed as a familiar deputy whose name she couldn't recall led him in. She stared at the man who had broken her heart. He was in a white dress shirt and tailored black pants, minus a tie and belt—ultra-conservative, tall, dark, and handsome. He was burned in her memory, but he wasn't as she remembered. God damn him, he looked even better.

She forced herself to swallow past the thick lump in her throat, her arms still pulled tightly across and over her stomach, as she made herself look away from the icy blue eyes she'd never expected to see again.

"Thank you," she said to the deputy as he removed the cuffs from a man who had hurt her. She heard the door vaguely over her thudding heart, and her unease lingered as she made herself look right at him. For the first time in her life, she couldn't come up with any words that would allow her to regain even a tiny shred of the dignity she'd lost to this man.

"I wasn't sure you'd come," Jack said. What was it about his deep voice? He had been able to talk her into anything, including having his ring on her finger before he turned around and kicked her to the curb.

"I shouldn't be here, considering the difficulties you caused me," she replied, though she didn't move any closer. Her voice already held a pissed-off edge. It was killing her to stand there so calmly. "Pretty sure, from the restraining order and the sheriff's last talk with me, where he reminded me to grow the fuck up, move on, and never come near you again, that this is a bad idea for me. But you know that already, so I can't help wondering why you called me. You killed someone, you said?"

He glanced to the door, and she took in his heavy five o'clock shadow. He rubbed both his wrists, rolling up his sleeves. His suit was cut elegantly, a tux. It looked as if it had been made for him, by the expense of the cloth. His fingers were bare, but then, the cops would have taken everything when they booked him.

"So they said, but it's not true. You look good." His blue eyes were frigid, icy, far different from hers. He jutted his chin toward her. "I see you're a redhead now."

She wasn't sure if he was mocking her, and she found herself reaching up to her hair, which was pulled back. She'd settled on the color a few years earlier. She had to fight to keep her self-doubts, which had kicked the shit out of her confidence, from resurfacing. No, she wouldn't let him do that to her again.

"Look, Jack, you didn't call me here to talk about the shade of my hair, so I can't help wondering why you did call me. This makes no sense to me. You shouldn't be that desperate for a lawyer. The phonebook is flooded with them, some really good bottom-feeders. Take your pick. I can't seriously be your only option. I'm very well aware of how you feel about me. Out of all the lawyers to call, why me?"

"Why not you?" Jack said. "You're a lawyer and you're good, and I need one."

She knew bullshit. The tension was so thick that her stomach churned, and for a moment, she thought she might be sick. She was furious that she couldn't feel the hate she needed to feel for him. "Right, so you call me? You know what I remember, Jack, is the day you left me. I stood there, eating my heart, as you packed a suitcase and walked out the door, and as you did, remember what you said to me?" She had to force the lump in her throat away as she swallowed. The moment had gutted her. She still remembered the way he'd spoken to her, as if she'd done the most awful of things.

The table was between them, and there was something about the way he stood there, so strong and tall. She wasn't sure what to make of his expression. Evidently, she'd never been able to read him, and obviously, he wasn't going to answer.

"Let me help you out, since this bullshit silence doesn't work for me. You told me not to contact you, that it was over, that I was a mistake. That's what I remember."

He'd stared at her as if he'd hated her. She'd never forget that look. It haunted her still, and so did the papers she'd been served, which were tucked in the bottom drawer of her desk underneath the velvet box that held his ring. Damn, she didn't understand why she'd kept it.

"What do you want me to say, Karen, that I'm sorry? That's not why I called you. I think you know you'd be the last person I'd call if there were another option for me." Wow, he really could sound like an asshole. "Look, I don't want to rehash our past, because it's done, over between us. The only thing I want—no, need is for you to get me out of this fucked-up situation. Don't you think it's convenient that all of this went down now, and I'm stuck in jail until I can go before a judge on Monday morning? Just get me out of here. Focus, come on, because female hysterics will solve nothing right now."

The dismissal in his tone was another reminder of how he seemed able to shut his feelings off with a flick of a switch. Karen let her arms fall to her sides, then fisted her hands, feeling a wave of anger. It was as if he couldn't understand how much he'd hurt her.

"You know, you need to work on your bedside manner. Because slapping me down again is only going to have me walking out of here." She took one step and then another, keeping her distance from him. "You were right about something in what you said to me: This relationship of ours has run its course. Now this, here, you calling me to come and…what, get you out of jail and off a murder charge I don't even know anything about? No, fuck off, Jack. Find yourself another lawyer. Although I empathize, I won't help you. I will not allow you to break my heart and fuck with me again. Remember the restraining order you managed to get against me? Well, it still exists, and here I am, breaking it. I still have it in my drawer at the office, kind of a reminder of how stupid I was. All you did was make a call, say I threatened you. Yeah, maybe I did in one of those hundreds of messages. Yet here you are, calling me. You killed someone? I don't get this." She was trembling. She made herself keep walking to the door, but Jack stepped in front of her.

"Please stop, Karen. You don't get it. You have every right to hate me, and I know I hurt you—but no, I didn't kill anyone!"

She took a step back, feeling his anger. She just didn't understand. Why was he calling her, of all people, to help him? Why had he walked away from her all those years earlier? Why had he done what he'd done? That was the one thing he'd never shared with her.

He pulled in a breath and ran his hand through his thick dark hair as if trying to steady himself. "All I can say, Karen, is I'm sorry, but at the time, it was the only thing I could do to see that you stayed away from me." He was shaking his head, and the emotion lingered between them. "I don't do something without a reason, and I certainly wouldn't be calling you for help, but the thing is, you're the only one who can help me out of the kind of trouble I'm in, the only one I can trust. You know me, Karen." The passion in his voice was so direct, but passion and heat had never been their problem.

"You're wrong," she said. "I don't really know you. How can I be the only one who can help you? That makes absolutely no sense, Jack. What is this, this game? Is this just something else to fuck with me, to fuck with my head? It's been a long time, and I've got a good thing going for myself. Why are you here, trying to mess with that?" She was leaning forward, breathing in and out. She hadn't realized she'd been yelling back at him.

He shut his eyes and exhaled. "Please, Karen, I'm not trying to mess with you. I wouldn't do that, not to you…" He inhaled roughly and glanced to the side. "This may sound absolutely crazy, but when I was arrested and heard the charges, the who, why, and where, all I could think of was calling you—even though I knew the best thing for you would be for me not to call. Please, Karen."

He lifted his gaze, and the expression was so raw and real, something she'd never seen before. Maybe he was messing with her, but she knew what she was going to say the moment she opened her mouth, though she tried to will it away.

"I hate you, Jack."

He nodded as if he understood. "And you have every right."

"Fine. I'll see what I can do to get you out. No promises. But then, and you listen to me, Jack, you find yourself another lawyer." She pounded a fist on the metal door. "Let me out," she snapped, and stepped back as it opened.

"Karen," Jack called out. She stopped and glanced back from the open doorway. The deputy had already stepped inside and was cuffing him again. "Thank you."

She didn't know what to say to him, so she only

nodded and kept walking through the stationhouse, to the front door, hearing voices and phones, knowing her brother was waiting outside. She'd just done the one thing she'd promised herself she wouldn't do: help a man who had destroyed her and broken her heart.

CHAPTER
Three

OWEN WASN'T WAITING outside the police station. In fact, he was waiting just inside the glassed-in waiting area at the front of the cop shop, and his eyes connected with hers as soon as she stepped out from the back.

Her heels clicked on the floor, and she said nothing as she walked straight for the doors without stopping and pushed them open. She couldn't get out of there fast enough. Very aware that her brother was right behind her, she strode down the concrete steps to the sidewalk and barely made it off the last step before she felt the churning in her stomach. She walked to the only bush out front just as her stomach pitched, and from out of nowhere, she vomited.

"Oh, man," Owen said from behind her, his hand on her back, as she spit and rested her hands on her knees, again pulling in a breath, shaky, trembling. When she stood up and pressed the back of her hand to her mouth, she couldn't avoid looking her brother's way.

"Come on," was all he said, his hand on her back, and

he somehow ushered her to his van, which was parked two stalls over.

She didn't allow her gaze to connect with a passing couple, who she knew had seen everything. Owen pulled open the door, and she climbed in the passenger seat of the older-model van. He stood there a second, taking her in, and she didn't know if the shock on his face meant he was going to lecture her or start in with all the questions she expected, the ones he hadn't yet asked.

"You okay?"

She pulled her hand over her mouth again, feeling the burn in her stomach and wanting water to rinse her mouth and maybe settle the queasiness, which she knew was just nerves. "I'm fine."

He swore under his breath and then closed her door and walked around. She reached for the seatbelt and fastened it, glad now that her brother had insisted on taking her to the station. Owen was right: She wasn't in any condition to drive.

He took his time putting his seatbelt on, putting the key in the ignition, and then starting the engine. "So I've been sitting out here, trying to wrap my head around the fact that you're married…"

"Was married, past tense." She wouldn't let him finish. "If you can call it that. Not sure it even counts, considering a job interview lasts longer." She could feel him watching her. Thankfully, he put the van in gear and backed up.

"Wow, seriously? Whether you were or still are married is just semantics, Karen. That's not the kind of thing you keep secret, and you just went and paid some guy we don't even know you married a jail visit to help him out of a jam. What kind of loser is he?" Owen's voice dripped with sarcasm as he pressed the gas, as if he'd understand anything about the situation.

Karen gripped the strap of the seatbelt over her shoulder. "Jack Curtis is his name. He's not a loser, but yes, he wants my help, at least to get him bail and out of jail, even after everything." She knew it wasn't laughter, the rude sound her brother made. At the same time, she was still reeling over what she'd agreed to do. "I don't know if I can do this, Owen." She turned her head, pressing her cheek into the seat back.

Her brother was on edge, of course, but he had nothing on her.

"Please don't tell anyone in the family," she said. "Not Mom, Ryan, Marcus, Suzanne, Luke…I don't want anyone to know. I'm not exactly proud of what happened, and then there was how I reacted."

"I think maybe you need to start at the beginning and tell me what the fuck you did, Karen. Like, what the hell? I just don't get it, but I'm thinking some pretty bad things. Who is this guy? You should have told us, told me."

She shut her eyes for another second, hoping it would steady her, but it didn't. "It was one of those things, you know. A stupid moment. We've all had them." She turned her head to watch her brother, who said nothing, looking straight ahead as he pulled up to a stop light. "I don't even know how it started. It just did. It was during law school, at the beginning, and there he was. Jack was everything I wasn't, and he knew what he wanted. He was smart, brilliant, confident. He had passed the bar and been offered a position at the DA's office. Everyone wanted him, including me. I thought I was the luckiest girl around because we spent every minute together. It started as hot courtroom sex. He was on the other side, and I was interning under the public defender. The first time, it was, like, a closet at the courthouse, his car in the parking lot, a…"

"Whoa, stop, for Christ's sake! I don't want to hear about your sex life. No details," Owen said, cutting her off.

It was too late, though. Every one of those memories hit her, the memories she hadn't allowed herself to think of in so long. The way he had touched her, kissed her, fucked her, it both saddened and angered her. It had been hot and dangerous, and he'd been like a drug to her. She had craved him, dreamed of him, loved him. How she hated him now.

"I never thought it was possible to love someone so much that I obsessed over him. You know, I can say it now. It's taken me how long…?" She took in the darkened highway, glad for it so she could sit and consider without the sun spotlighting the one part of her life that had been so damn messy.

"I don't know how long, Karen, because you didn't tell us—didn't tell me. Why not? Seriously."

She turned her head to her brother again, hearing how pissed he was and how personally he was taking this. "Because it was over as quick as it started. One minute we hadn't even dated. It was just sex, great sex. Then we were on a road trip in Georgia, a backroads place, and he suggested getting married. Next thing, we were standing in front of a justice of the peace, and he was slipping this ring on my finger, you know the fake metal and glass kind? He picked one up at the corner store.

"Then two days later, he was walking out of his apartment with a suitcase and telling me to fuck off. What the hell was I to think? I thought he was crazy, messing with me. But it was the way he looked at me, with such hate, as if I'd done something. I mean, I loved him." She pressed her hand to her chest. Owen dragged a hand over his face, and she could hear the scrape of whiskers in the silence that lingered. "He got a restraining order against me, considering I didn't handle it too well," she continued.

Owen shot her a look. Of course, he was shocked. She was still humiliated by what had happened. "You're serious."

"He told me it was over, but I just wouldn't let it go. I mean, we were married, for the love of God. So I called him over and over, filled his voicemail to the point his mailbox was full every day. I didn't stop. I kept phoning, feeling absolutely gutted. I mean, who does that, marries you and then walks out on you and refuses to talk to you? Well, you know me. I wasn't taking that. I don't even remember the content of my messages, but I'm pretty sure they were filled with dire warnings and threats of bodily harm, because next thing, I was served a restraining order. What made it worse was that it was Sheriff Bert who paid me a visit and gave me a sit-down, a dose of reality. He said Jack didn't want to be contacted, that I'd made my point, and that I'd gone too far. It was humiliating."

"And Marcus doesn't know?"

She breathed in past the ache, feeling the sting of that moment from so long ago, sitting there in a chair with Bert giving her a look that let her know she'd really messed up big time. She wished she could go back and undo what had happened. "Marcus had just started, you know. He was still a green deputy. Bert promised he wouldn't say anything. At the same time, he made me promise to stop calling Jack, or I could find myself behind bars, and the law degree I'd given everything for would be gone. Jack had changed his number, so it was an easy promise to make. I couldn't call him anymore because I didn't know where he was or how to get a hold of him. So I swallowed it, and…"

Her brother was pulling his hand over his face again, shaking his head. Yeah, evidently, he was having some trouble getting his head around this. "Marcus has been with the sheriff's office going on eight years."

"Just over."

He nodded. "You were just a kid, then. You're saying it was that long ago?"

She shrugged, because the problem was that although it was so long ago, it felt like yesterday.

"Wow, that sounds totally fucked up, Karen."

Yes, and her brother had no idea how much. "I know," she said, "especially considering I have to go back and see him."

He slammed on the brakes and swerved to the side of the highway, and she jerked forward, grateful that it was dark in the cab between them. "You just finished telling me that this guy fucked you over big time and has a restraining order on you, and you're going back to—"

"Just one time, Owen, just to get him out, if I can, and that's it. I told Jack that's all I'm willing to do. Then he has to find himself another lawyer."

Owen let out a rude sound under his breath as he put the van back in gear and pulled back on the highway, shaking his head. "You know, Karen, sometimes you can be your own worst enemy."

She turned her head, looking out into the darkness, feeling the sting of his words. She felt a tear slip out and roughly wiped it away. "You think I don't know that? But what kind of lawyer would I be if I couldn't put personal feelings aside?"

"Well, you just keep telling yourself that, Karen. I guess I don't understand why you married him, why he walked out, why you have a restraining order against you. That entire story makes no sense. He didn't want to see you or talk to you, yet here he is, calling you, and you go running to him."

She made herself look straight ahead. "How am I supposed to explain something I can't even understand? God dammit, now I sound like one of my clients."

She realized in that second that if she'd heard the same story from another woman, she'd have told her to get her head right. But after all these years, the same question still haunted her: What had she done to have him walking out the door?

"You get anything to eat tonight?" Owen said. So he was done talking about it.

"You're doing it again, Owen, trying to father me—but I'm a big girl, and…"

"And you just had the rug yanked out from under you. You were puking your guts out over a guy who, by the sounds of it, has totally and completely conned you. I don't understand any of it. You should eat, and you need to tell everyone. No more secrets, Karen. I mean, do you know the details of what he did? Maybe he's guilty and you shouldn't be helping him. Talk to Marcus. Get him to look into it."

Karen took in the brother who had been there for all of them. At the same time, it seemed no one had ever thought to check in on him and see how he was.

"Not yet," she replied. She knew she was being stubborn. "And how about we stop talking about me and talk about you? Before Jack called, you showed up at my office, and I can't help wondering if there's something going on with you. You sound off, or you did."

He made another rude sound and shook his head, but he didn't pull his gaze from the road as he drove. "We're talking about you, Karen, your problem. Don't start spinning this and shining anything my way, because we aren't done by a longshot. You're in over your head. I don't know this guy, none of us do, but either you tell Marcus or I will."

There it was, the tough love. Owen had stepped in too many times after their dad had left, after her world had fallen apart.

"Don't push, Owen. I'll think about it."

"You do that, Karen, but a word of advice? Don't think too long, because from where I'm sitting, you're being dragged into the middle of something that could end up hurting you. Family is family, Karen. I'll give you tonight, and then tomorrow, you call Marcus."

CHAPTER
Four

LATE NIGHTS, bad coffee, and impossible cases were what Karen had always associated with being a big-city lawyer. Maybe that was why she'd decided to go it alone in the small town of Livingston, where she could be responsible only to herself. Or maybe, if she were being completely honest, she had stayed in Livingston because it was the only way to protect the part of her that had been hurt so badly by Jack Curtis.

Now here he was, back in her life, and what was she doing? Helping him, the man she'd given her heart to, the same man who, in one blinding moment, had kicked her to the curb as he walked out. This was the very definition of lunacy.

Her cell phone buzzed as she worked her expensive espresso machine and yawned. She'd somehow managed four hours of sleep after sitting in the dark, staring at the ceiling as her worry ran rampant. Karen put her mug down and stared at the text from Owen on her phone: *Call Marcus this morning!*

"Stop pushing, Owen..." she muttered as she looked

around her condo. The morning light spilled through the window, reflecting off the gleaming white cabinets and countertop of her open-concept kitchen. The walls were white, and the furniture was practical. The light blue sectional was still covered with a cream throw blanket, in a heap from where she'd fallen asleep sometime before dawn. The coffee table was scattered with a notepad, crumpled paper, and what she had come up with as a plan of action to get Jack out of jail.

She still didn't have a clue about any of the details, the what, where, and why that surrounded Jack's arrest, or who he was accused of killing. She needed the police report, the evidence. Her brother Marcus would have access to the kinds of information that, for a lawyer, would either make or break a case. But then she'd have to tell him, and right now, she was putting that off as long as she could.

She turned back to the espresso machine and turned the dial, letting the steam whirr as she filled a mug. There was a knock at her door. She flicked off the machine and carried the mug, now filled with a long dark brew, with her as she strode barefoot, wearing a bulky white T-shirt and sweatpants. She rose on her tiptoes and looked through the peephole, seeing her sister, Suzanne.

Karen flicked the lock and pulled open the door. "Why are you here?" she said, noting Suzanne's tidy blue firefighter's uniform, her dark hair hiked back high in a ponytail.

Suzanne stepped past Karen into her condo. "Owen called this morning, said he dropped you off at home last night and your car is still at work. Said you may need a ride. You have coffee on? Because I didn't have time to grab any this morning. Was planning on getting some at the firehouse…"

She was still talking from the kitchen. All Karen could

do was give her door a shove closed as she listened to her sister rummaging through her cupboards. Karen just lifted her mug and took a swallow, hoping to clear the cobwebs from her head as she stared at the notes and papers that covered her coffee table.

"I still can't believe you bought this fancy coffee machine," Suzanne said, already working it, having made herself at home, just like all her family did when they dropped by. There was just something about all of them, as if they knew no boundaries.

"So Owen called you this morning and said…?" Karen started. She let it linger. Her voice was raspy, likely from lack of sleep.

Suzanne tossed her a glance over her shoulder as she made herself an espresso, the noise of the machine welcome in the quiet room. "Said you'd need a ride to the office. Apparently, he had a call at the crack of dawn, some emergency plumbing situation, busted pipes or something, and couldn't get you. I said I'd stop by on my way to the station. By the looks of you, you need to shake a leg and throw some clothes on. I'm pulling the early shift today, so I can't linger. You look tired. You work late?"

What was she supposed to say? "You could say that. New case. Trying to figure out the where, the when, and the how—you know. But Owen shouldn't have called you. I can throw on a pair of sneakers and walk the few blocks to my car. The fresh air will do me good."

"You sure?" Suzanne said. "Because it sounded to me like it was important. Owen also said there was something you needed to tell all of us and that I should make a point of asking."

She curled her fingers around her mug, then lifted it and took another swallow. She let out a rough laugh and gave her head a shake. "Asshole," she muttered under her breath.

Suzanne gestured toward her with her mug of coffee. "Hmm, take it we're talking about Owen? Now I'm really curious. Something going on?" She lifted her wrist and looked at her watch while taking another swallow of coffee. "I need to get going, so how about telling me what's what? You know I'll likely find out anyway."

Karen just stared at her sister, who had inherited the same tall and lanky frame as her brothers, coming in at five foot seven. Karen, meanwhile, was the same five foot nothing as their mom and had inherited the curves Suzanne hadn't. "I did something years ago that's coming back to haunt me."

Suzanne froze with the mug of coffee halfway to her mouth. Her blue eyes widened. "And I take it this is something Owen knows?" It wasn't a question, but Karen knew Suzanne wouldn't let it drop. "Come on. Spill, Karen! Rip the Band-Aid off. Tell me. You know nothing you did could surprise me, considering all the trouble you looked for and found. I still wonder how you emerged unscathed…"

"I was married," Karen said, cutting her sister off.

Suzanne's jaw dropped, and she stilled, becoming very quiet, which was unusual for her.

"Owen knows only because he showed up at my office and was there when he called—Jack, my husband. He's found himself in jail. Owen drove me to Sweetwater County, where he's behind bars. You're right, I do need to get my car, because I need to go back and see him. I said I would help him, at least get him out on bail if I can. Owen believes I should tell everyone, but you know what? There's so much about my relationship and history with Jack that I don't want to talk about. I don't want to have any of you looking at me like you are now, seeing me as a fuck-up and adding in your two cents about what was I thinking, and how could I? Those are the same things I've said to myself over and over. I just don't want to hear it." Karen leaned in, pulling one arm over her stomach and squeezing the handle of her mug.

Suzanne made a face and shrugged. "I could never see you as a fuck-up." She rested her mug on the counter after taking another big swallow and glancing at her watch again. "Well, I need to get to the station, but let me know, will you, when you plan on telling everyone the story? Because I want to be there and hear every one of the juicy details you'll be forced to spill. I might even bring popcorn. Wow, married, you?" It was mocking. Suzanne was shaking her head, laughing under her breath as she walked to the door. She pulled it open and glanced back to Karen. "Oh, I take it you don't want a ride?"

Karen tossed her a long, lingering look. "No, I don't need a ride."

Suzanne was still laughing as she stepped out and pulled the door closed, and Karen heard her phone ding. When she reached for it, she took in the text. It was Suzanne, already prying for more.

So when, where, and how? Like…holy shit, sister! Details, please! I'm not sure I can wait until later. The suspense… Damn, girl!

Karen tossed the phone back on the counter, feeling her carefully concealed secret spiraling out of control, much like she had opened Pandora's box, and every secret, every carefully crafted lie, would be out there for everyone to see.

CHAPTER

Five

KAREN TOOK in the Sweetwater County sheriff's office and jail. She'd been inside too many times to count, but something about sitting parked out front in her practical Honda that morning had been different. Scratch that. Everything about the situation had shifted from business to far too personal. To make it worse, she still didn't understand why Jack had called her—and why now? Eight years was a long time.

A tap on her window had her jumping, pressing her hand to her heart as she flicked her gaze to the glass. Her brother Marcus, in his sheriff's uniform, was leaning down to her window, but it took her another second to reach for the handle and open it.

Marcus rested his hand on the door frame. "Sorry, didn't mean to scare you. What are you doing here?" Everything in his expression was curious and all cop, though his shades hid his O'Connell blue eyes.

As she stepped out, wearing black pumps and a navy skirt with a white sleeveless silky blouse, she took her time, considering what to say. Her paranoia was in overdrive.

Maybe Owen had once again sent Marcus her way. He really did know how to get under her skin.

"You have a client in jail here?" her brother added when she didn't answer.

"So to speak. What are you doing down this way? Out of your jurisdiction, aren't you, Marcus? And I thought you didn't work weekends?"

"I work all the time. That's kind of what being a sheriff is: When someone calls, I'm there. Just here now for a local theft that's crossed a couple county lines. Oh, and Owen sent me an odd text. Said you were trying to get a hold of me?"

Damn you, Owen! She wondered what expression was on her face by the way Marcus watched her, so she forced herself to look away, giving her head a shake. "Owen shouldn't have bothered you."

Marcus towered over her. She hated having to look up. He rested his arm on the top of her Honda while she reached into the back seat for her briefcase, then closed the door. "Okay…what gives?" he said, then let out a rough laugh. She could see his amusement. "You and Owen butting heads over something?"

If only it were that simple.

"Just a big brother who can't mind his own business, is all," she replied.

Marcus pulled his shades down his nose and let out a rough laugh, peering at her. "Come on, Karen. This is me, remember."

She was positive she held her breath, then had to look away to the jail, knowing Jack and her brother could never meet. This secret was becoming more and more difficult to keep.

"Can you do me a favor and find out information on a client of mine? The name is Jack Curtis. I need the details surrounding why he was charged with murder, who he killed, what they have on him…you know, all the usual dirt. I need to find out what you all have against my client so I can figure out a way to save his ass."

She wanted to pat herself on the back. Right, just treat him like every other client. This was business—even though she'd been married to the man, and he had a restraining order out against her, yet there she was, walking into a jail for him. There were way too many questions surrounding all of it.

"Your client has been arrested and you didn't get the police report?" Marcus frowned.

Okay, maybe she needed to add a little more. He didn't even try to hide his confusion.

"Well, the call came in late last night, you know, and…" She started walking.

Marcus rested his hand on her arm to stop her. "You know I can do that, but why do I get the feeling there's something else?" His hand was still on her arm, and she took in how serious he now seemed. Marcus was perceptive, always had been. Maybe that was why he was a damn good cop.

"You know, I'd rather not say," she replied.

Marcus inclined his head, pulled his shades off, and tucked them in his shirtfront. "Why?"

Okay, why the hell hadn't she just said it was nothing? Now she had a curious Marcus who wasn't going to let it drop. "What is it with you and Owen, always pushing?" she snapped. "Fine, here it is. You want all the dirt? Yes, it's about my client inside, who called me last night…but I was married to him." She lifted her hand and swept it to the jail, maybe because she couldn't think of what else to do upon seeing his shock. "Your face says everything. That's why I didn't want to share any of my personal screw-ups.

It was a really long time ago, a blip. We were married, and then he was gone, walking out the door, telling me to piss off. It was over as quick as it started. Oh, right, and then there's the matter of the restraining order he had against me—something about me threatening him in one of the more than two hundred messages I left.

"Sheriff Bert actually tracked me down when I was just about to start clerking for Judge Thompson, just finishing with the public defender's office. We had a sit-down, or rather, he made me sit. Just FYI, this was when you were still a green deputy and had just started working for the sheriff's office, so that should give you an idea that this all happened in another lifetime. I was kind of like you back then, always finding trouble. Sheriff Bert felt the need to step in because of how far off the rails I had gone. He basically informed me how badly this was all going to play out for me if I didn't get my shit together and leave the guy be, but then, when a guy marries you and then tells you to fuck off two days later, what's a girl to do?"

She knew she was being dramatic, and it had all spilled out. She never in a million years had expected to tell him everything. She'd never seen this look on Marcus's face before, not for her, anyway. "Right, okay then," she said. "Good talk. Now, listen. If you have any questions, don't ask, because I don't want to discuss it, and I really need to get inside now and see this man I never expected to see again. So if you don't mind…" She gripped the handle of her briefcase and started to turn when Marcus slapped a hand on her arm, holding her where she was.

"What the fuck, Karen?" Oh, there it was. "Yeah, I do mind. Are you kidding me?" He let out a rough laugh, but she knew he was trying to get his head around her little bomb. "I don't even know where to begin."

She allowed her gaze to drop to her brother's hand,

which was still on her arm, before he pulled it away and ran it roughly over his face, then made a rude noise. "Well, that makes two of us," she said. "Look, Marcus, I can see you have a few things to say on the matter and are likely trying to find the words. Well, there aren't any. It's done, it's over, and I never told anyone in the family because it's one of those mortifying things where someone turns out to be the type of person you never thought he could be. I never wanted you to know—or anyone. If Owen had just minded his own business instead of pushing..." She gestured to the front door and up the steps to the sheriff's office, and Marcus nodded.

"Go, but I want to talk to you about this." His expression was grim.

She wished he would drop it, but she knew that wasn't going to happen, so she just nodded back. "Fine, but no inquisition."

This time, she thought the amused grin on his face might be humor. As she started up the concrete steps, breathing a sigh of relief that he wasn't tagging along, he called out, "Karen?"

She stopped with her hand on the door, about to pull it open. "What, Marcus?"

His hands were on his hips before he moved to put his shades back on. "This guy sounds like a piece of work. I don't know the whole story, but I plan to hear it, and I have to ask, why are you helping him?"

There it was, the million-dollar question.

She just stared at her brother, wishing some words of wisdom would come to her. "I wish I could tell you, Marcus," was all she said.

Before her brother could add one more thing, she pulled open the door to the Sweetwater County sheriff's office, where Jack was currently parked in a cell. She hoped for a lot of things, namely an answer to why he'd cut her out of his life in such a cruel way, treating her as if she were nothing, as if she'd done something horrible. She didn't understand anything about that day, how he'd loved her in the morning and then, hours later, hated her as he walked out the door.

———

KAREN SQUEEZED her pen as she sat in the metal chair at the metal table, listening to the clang of the steel door. She scribbled Jack's name and the date on a pad of yellow legal paper in an attempt to steady her already frayed nerves.

She lifted her head as a deputy she'd seen with Marcus a few times brought Jack in. His heavy five o'clock shadow was darker, and his white shirt was heavily wrinkled. She was aware he was definitely not in comfortable accommodations and was likely sharing a bench with a number of other arrestees waiting out the weekend in a concrete cell.

"Thank you," she forced herself to say to the deputy, who only nodded to her before leaving. Karen gestured to the empty chair until Jack pulled it out, and the scrape over the concrete was welcome in the silence.

"So you slept well, I see," she said, forcing sharpness into her tone. She clicked her pen, unable to think of what else to write on the paper, and looked up at a man she wished she could feel nothing for.

"I've been in worse places," Jack said. "I guess I should say thanks for coming back. I half expected you to tell me to go fuck myself. It's what I deserve."

Her heart was thumping, and she could feel her nerves getting the best of her. He let his gaze linger on her, and she didn't have a clue what he was thinking. "So we should start with who you killed…"

"I didn't kill anyone. I told you that already." He crossed his arms over his solid chest, striking, handsome, athletic. She had to look away, as the old adage about improving with age absolutely applied to him.

"You should know that's not the issue," she said. "Come on, Jack. You're a lawyer, too. I shouldn't have to explain this. You've found yourself arrested because there's evidence to the contrary, so if you want my help, start by telling me everything. I have no police report yet, so I want to hear whatever they think they have on you. Don't leave anything out, because I will be going through the report. I expect to have it before I leave here today." She jabbed her pen his way as if emphasizing her point. "I know you know the law and how things work. You're a smart man, Jack, but you've managed to land yourself in something here."

"You know, it's different when you're on the other side of it," he said. "Everything you know about the law, everything you tell people who are sitting in the same spot I'm in right now…well, all of it suddenly isn't so black and white. Right to business, huh?"

For a second, she didn't know what to say. She felt herself pulling back. "You're not seriously going to do the 'Hey, how are you? It's great to see you' thing, are you? Because if you do, I'll walk out of here, and you can find yourself another lawyer. Remember, we're not friends. You hate me, not that I have a clue as to why. So let's keep this to business."

There was something empowering about the fury she had suddenly summoned. It felt so good. But nonetheless, a smile pulled at the corners of his lips. Damn, was he fucking with her?

"You know what? On second thought," she said, scraping back her chair, "you *should* find yourself another lawyer. I shouldn't be here. I'm very well aware of how you treated me, and now you suddenly want my help?" She flicked her pen and grabbed the pad of paper to stuff it into the briefcase at her feet.

"Whoa, hang on a second, here. I've done some things I'm not proud of, Karen, and one of them is hurting you. I'm sorry. One day, I hope to make you understand that it wasn't… There was more to it. It wasn't that simple."

"Simple, what the fuck? You crushed me, told me we were done. You married me, and then you wouldn't take my calls…"

"I know what I did," he snapped, cutting her off. "Look, can we table this for now? Aside from how I screwed everything up with you, the imminent problem, as you can see, is that I'm in jail, with a murder charge hanging over my head."

She had to pull in a breath at the passion emanating from him now. How had she forgotten his passion?

He seemed to steady himself as he sat back, but she could still see how tense he was as he looked around, up to a camera in the corner, which she knew would be off, and then back to her. "Look, everything about this story will sound crazy, I know—but I'm charged with the murder of a woman who was found in a hotel room booked under my name. The thing is, I didn't book the hotel. I didn't kill her. I had never even been there, yet they said my things were there, my clothes, personal items. I have no idea what they found. I only know I'm behind bars, charged with murder. All I can think is that I somehow pissed off the wrong person. Someone went out of his way to pin something on me. It was elaborate. Whoever it was went to great lengths…"

She was shaking her head. "Stop. Just stop, Jack. Are you telling me you don't know this woman, or you do?"

He pulled his hand roughly over his face and shook his

head, leaning forward on the table. "I do know her," he said, and something in his expression had her feeling a jealousy she didn't want.

"How well?" she said, unable to stop herself. "Never mind. I don't want to know." She was furious because she shouldn't be feeling this way. How many years had it been? Yet she was still hanging on.

"Look, she's someone who is—*was* important to me. We were involved, seeing each other, lovers." He gestured vaguely, not looking at her.

She didn't think she wanted to hear any more. She forced herself to breathe in, breathe out, and she didn't miss how unsettled he looked as he glanced at her and away again. "Lovers, really? You mean your girlfriend? Doesn't look good for you, Jack." She pulled her arms over her chest, feeling strange.

He didn't shake his head or try to correct her. "We were involved, not seriously, but I cared about her. She was important to me. But I don't know why she'd be here in Sweetwater County, in a hotel down in Big Timber. She doesn't even know anyone here. When she called me, I thought she was passing through or something because she was having car trouble. I called her back, but she didn't answer, so I started driving, more than two hundred miles, before I was pulled over. Next I know, after they asked for my ID, the cops were coming in, lights flashing, a gun in my face. I was hauled out of my car, forced to lie face down on the concrete on the highway, and cuffed. Now here I am. Yeah, I lawyered up as soon as I heard Bonnie was dead in a roadside hotel and my things were there..." He lifted his hands. Either he was a fabulous actor, or he really was thrown by all of this.

"So you were driving here?" She gestured with her pen.

"That's what I said."

"No, actually, you didn't say where you were driving until now. Or that you were pulled over on the highway."

He pressed his hands over his face and swiped down, and she could see his frustration. "Look, Karen, can you get a copy of the police report and the crime scene photos? There has to be something in there to clear this up. No one is telling me anything, and all I have is the little that was said to me."

Karen shook her head, then flicked her gaze over to Jack. "Okay, you know what? This does sound unbelievable, and it has too many holes. So my question to you is what is this really about? Did you figure you'd have one more go at me, see how gullible I still am?"

"I'm telling the truth, Karen. I'm not a liar."

She pulled back, and maybe her disgust showed in her face. "I wouldn't know. Apparently, I'm not a very good judge of character, especially of the man I married. Would you lie?" She shrugged. "Did you lie to me?"

There she went, the road she'd promised herself she wouldn't go down. This was the first time she'd ever seen him look so uncertain.

"Okay, you know what?" she continued. "Scratch that. Maybe you did lie. Maybe you get off on reeling women in and playing with their emotions. The thing about me, and what sets us apart, is that I keep my word. I said I would help you get bail, but then you need to find another lawyer, because I'm no longer a naive young woman who'll follow you anywhere and believe blindly some bullshit story…"

"Look, Karen, there're just some things you don't know—"

"Yet here I am," she snapped, cutting him off, leaning back in the uncomfortable steel chair, gesturing with arms wide. "You want my help? Then you're going to have to level with me. I don't have time for this secrecy bullshit. You say you don't lie, that things were planted, that you were driving here… That's ridiculous. I won't be played, not by you, not ever again. What are you not telling me?"

His hand was reaching for hers, covering it. "Karen…"

She didn't like feeling that warmth, so she yanked her hand back. He was uncomfortable; she could tell by the way he fisted his hand as he watched her.

"You want the truth?"

She inclined her head. "Please." Her voice dripped with sarcasm. He had to be working an angle.

"I haven't allowed myself to care about another woman in a long time," he said. "I did once, and, well… You haven't met my family, but let's just say the reason we're not together is the same reason Bonnie was murdered. I cared about her very much, and that was my mistake."

Karen pulled her arms over her chest, feeling the knot in her stomach once again.

Jack continued. "All I can guess is that someone on the outside is manipulating things, pulling the strings, messing with my life once again."

"I've heard better stories, more believable."

The fire in his blue eyes flickered.

She lifted a hand. "Okay, let's just say what you're saying is true. Answer me this: Why would someone do that?"

He was shaking his head. "You don't get it, Karen. This was a setup. How do you take out your enemy? How do you keep someone in line? How do you silence a problem? I wasn't there at the hotel. It's nearly three hours to get here, and I was on my way." He glanced away again and let out a heavy sigh.

She didn't have a clue whether he was messing with

her, lying to her, but something lingered in that second between them. "Dressed in a tux?" She gestured with her pen. "Yes, I've noticed what you're wearing."

He shut his eyes and ran his hand through his dark hair, which was a mess. She sensed his frustration. "The tux was for a black-tie charity event. Bonnie was supposed to go with me. She was supposed to meet me. I took off early that afternoon to do a couple of things before getting ready. I had a voicemail from her. She was in trouble. Her car had broken down. There was just something in her voice… I didn't keep the voicemail. I mean, why would I?" He glanced back at her. "Look, I know how the law works, and whoever did kill Bonnie does, as well. I don't have the crime scene details, the photos, or any clue as to why they think it was me, but I have a pretty good idea how it was done."

She made herself take a second as she considered what else to say. "Very cloak and dagger, Jack. What the hell am I supposed to do with this? Why me? Why drag me into this?" she started, then made herself stop. "You know what? Don't answer that." She grabbed her briefcase and shoved the notepad and pen inside as she scooted back her chair, taking in how quiet he was. She needed to tell him to go fuck himself and find another lawyer, but she couldn't get the words past her lips. She was halfway to the door when she heard his chair scrape.

"Karen, I don't trust many people, but you're one I do. I knew you were here," he said. "I've always known where you were. Don't you want to know why I walked out on you that day, why I said what I did? You haven't demanded that I explain. Maybe I expected that from you."

She stopped. Wanting to know was the reason she had a restraining order against her. She pounded on the door until the deputy opened it, then said, "I'm done here."

As the deputy stepped in, over to a man she thought she'd never get over, Karen just looked at him. "You know what? At one time, yeah, I wanted to know. But considering everything…no, I don't anymore," she said, then started out of the room.

"So who's the liar now?" she heard him call out, but she forced herself to keep going, putting one foot in front of the other, squeezing the handle of her briefcase, wondering how much the deputy knew of her and Jack and her relationship to him.

She spotted Marcus talking with the Sweetwater County sheriff, and both men glanced her way. Her brother said something she couldn't make out, and the sheriff was now walking into his office. Marcus held the door open for her.

"You all done?" he asked.

She didn't miss the file he was holding as she walked through. "I am," was all she could make herself say. She strode down the concrete steps in her heels, her brother behind her, staring straight ahead to her Honda.

"Hold up a second." Marcus had his hand on her arm again, and she turned at the bottom of the concrete steps. He held out the file, looking grim. "This guy, Jack Curtis, is bad news. You were really married to him?"

She took the file. "You read it?"

Marcus glanced out to the road. "Yeah. When you read everything in there, I want you to tell him to find someone else to represent him. Oh, and Mom called when you were meeting with Mr. Curtis. Apparently, Owen texted her, saying we're having a family barbecue tonight because you have news to share."

She could feel the knot in her stomach again as she stared at Marcus. "Owen," was all she could get out.

Marcus raised a brow but didn't smile. "Well, think of

it this way, Karen. This makes it easy. With us all in one place, you can tell everyone, get it over with."

She gripped the file and her briefcase, trying to get her tongue to move, but all she could get out was a sigh, knowing Marcus meant well.

"And, Karen, I'm not kidding about telling this guy to find someone else."

She rested her briefcase on the hood of her Honda and shoved the file in. "Let me remind you of something, Marcus. You're a sheriff in Livingston. I don't tell you how to do your job, who to arrest or give a slap on the wrist, or a ticket, or a warning. So don't tell me how to do mine. That includes who I help or don't help. But thanks for the file." She gestured to her briefcase as she pulled open the door.

"Karen," he said again, still standing in front of her car, his hand on his duty belt, leveling that all-cop gaze her way.

"Oh my God, seriously, Marcus?" she snapped, frustration burning inside her.

"Be careful," was all he said, "and see you tonight."

She sighed, feeling the tension in her shoulders, and watched as her brother walked over to his cruiser and climbed in. She wanted to read the file and see what damning information and evidence were in there. How in the hell was she going to get out of seeing her family tonight?

CHAPTER

Six

KAREN CHECKED her phone after yet another ding. First had been her mom, who'd said dinner at six, then Suzanne, who'd said she couldn't wait to hear the news, then Marcus, who'd said there'd been a change of plans, and the barbecue would be at his place, then Ryan, who'd suggested his place. All she wanted to do was whack her head against a wall and scream at her family.

"Like, pick a place already!" she said out loud in frustration.

A knock at the door had her dragging her gaze up from the police file with the details of Jack's crime. A woman was dead, and to anyone else, it would've appeared an open and shut case. She still didn't have a clue who Jack Curtis really was—a psychopath, or had he been set up, as he'd claimed?

She let out a sigh as she took in the photos of his clothes, the woman, the hotel, and the evidence. "Coming," she called out and slapped the file closed. She slid off the stool at the kitchen island and strode barefoot to the door, still in her pencil skirt and silky blouse, wanting to grab a shower and change. She knew her family would show up there if she tried to blow them off.

She was on her tiptoes at the door, looking out the peephole, when she spotted Owen. She leaned her forehead against the door and let out a sigh before she stepped back, flicked open the deadbolt, and pulled the door open. "Well, look who's here: my brother, who can't keep his damn mouth shut."

Owen somehow moved her aside and stepped inside, shaking his head.

"Hey, Karen, how are you?" she said mockingly as she shoved the door closed. "Sorry for being such an asshole. Can I come in and apologize?"

He, though, being Owen, did nothing other than take in her living room, the pale greens, the nice touches. She was reminded of something from the night before.

"Really?" he said. "Look, change of plans. I'm sure you've heard tonight has moved to Mom's."

She just stared at him. "I thought it was at Ryan's now. I can't keep track of the half a dozen changes you've all made."

"Doesn't matter to me where it is, but Mom called and said Luke is on his way home. He just called, so you know what that means."

Right, her brother would be at their mom's, and it would be several days, depending on what he'd seen and done off in whatever shithole place he'd been shipped to, before he managed to get his head together enough to go out and somehow fit in with their friends and neighbors again.

"Okay, so it's at Mom's, then." She lifted her hands and couldn't explain the tightness in her chest. "Anyone else talk to him?" she added, wondering why Owen looked so off.

"No, but we'll see him tonight. You about ready?"

She leaned forward, lifting her watch. "It's, like, four o'clock…"

He was still watching her, and there it was, that over-protectiveness, along with something else.

"You know," she said, "when you came looking for me last night at the office, I couldn't help wondering if something was going on with you, something you wanted to talk about, before all hell blew up in my face, with Jack showing up. Is something going on?"

Owen wasn't looking at her, instead staring at everything on the island, the file Marcus had retrieved for her, which she was still trying to wrap her head around. "Nothing important," he said, then turned to her. "Right now, I'm kind of worried about you. Knowing you, Karen, I didn't want you getting lost and going to the wrong house, not when you have a family waiting to hear all the details about this husband of yours."

"Not my husband anymore, remember?" she said. "And why are you texting everyone behind my back like we're teenagers, anyway? It's like you're trying to force my hand, and I don't like it. You know, maybe I didn't want everyone to know what I did. It's embarrassing. Did you ever think of that? Have you never done something you plan never to share with anyone, to take to your grave?"

Owen didn't pull his gaze from her. In fact, he crossed his arms and seemed to really settle into his stance, but again, she couldn't help but think she'd hit a nerve. "You know, Karen, you really have a good thing going, here. You're a really good lawyer. You have a heart of gold, and you give two hundred percent to those you're trying to help. But while you went to law school in Missoula and came home on weekends, I was doing what I could to keep an eye on everyone. Marcus finally got his shit together, which is an absolute fucking miracle, because I expected him to end up behind bars, but he's finally on the right side of the law. Ryan jumped in there too as a ranger, and I still think that's because of Marcus. Those two could have ended up sharing a cell, always in trouble, doing everything together. Luke…well, I never knew what the hell was going on with him, but when he enlisted the day he was old enough, I wasn't surprised. Then there's Suzanne. Remember all the occupations she went through before deciding to be an EMT?"

"She's not an EMT, Owen. She's a firefighter."

"Yeah, but also an EMT. Anyway, the point is that she was, like, a hairdresser, a server, a bartender, a store clerk…"

"So what does this have to do with you forcing my hand?"

"Because you should have told us. Do you have any idea what it's been like, having to step up like I did? One day I was a sixteen-year-old, dating and just messing around, and then all of a sudden, Dad was gone and I had to grow up, because every one of you was looking to me. Mom couldn't do it all."

For a second, she didn't know what to say. She'd never heard her brother talk like this. She thought he sounded angry—at her, at all of them? "You're not okay," she said.

"You're right, I'm not," he said. "I'm pissed off over the fact you felt you couldn't say anything to me. Me, Karen. I should have been your go-to."

Now she felt like crap. She ran her hand over the back of her neck, and she couldn't figure out how to say sorry.

"So, if you don't mind, let's go," Owen said. "I'll drive, and you figure out what you're going to say to everyone. Don't worry about however much you want to drink. Have a few glasses of wine, liquid courage or whatever the hell you want to call it, but just tell everyone. No more secrets, because they have a way of eating you up inside. So, are you ready?" He seemed so distracted, and pushy, too.

She took in the closed file, which she really needed to dig into. She thought about the woman Jack had known, Bonnie, and how she'd been found dead, face down in that motel room, a bullet in the back of her head. Karen didn't think she'd ever get the image out of her mind. At the same time, it didn't look good for Jack. She considered another second before seeing Owen waiting impatiently, trying to settle her mind, knowing her brother was only trying to help.

"Sure, just let me grab a sweater."

KAREN STOOD in the doorway of her mom's house, the one she'd grown up in, and took her time slipping off her pumps. Her feet were aching. Thankfully, Owen was nowhere in sight. Luke was drinking a beer, sitting in the same spot he always did at their mom's, on the corner of the sofa, his back to the wall so he could see everyone coming and going. He didn't pull his gaze from her, his look far too perceptive. His hair was shorter, shoulder length, but appeared wet as if he'd just climbed out of the shower.

"Luke, you just get in?" she said.

"Not long ago," he replied.

She heard voices from the kitchen: her mom, Charlotte, Jenny, Suzanne, Ryan. Just then, little five-year-old Eva came running, her dark hair pulled back in a ponytail, wearing blue jeans and a white shirt. She wrapped her arms around Karen's bare leg.

"Hey, you!" Karen said. She hugged Eva. She was a

sweet little girl, so tiny. She knew Marcus and Charlotte loved her. They all did. "Heard you got your very own bunk bed. So where are you sleeping, top or bottom?"

"The bottom. You should come and see it. You could have a sleepover too, just like Alison."

"You know what?" Karen said. "I will. This week I'll come and see it, and you can definitely count me in on the sleepover—but you take the top, and I'll take the bottom."

Alison, her other niece, had called Eva from the kitchen and was now walking down the hall, coming their way. She was starting to look like a normal, well-adjusted teen. Her brown hair was shoulder length, and the nose ring was long gone. Karen couldn't remember having seen her eyes coated with all that heavy black makeup for a while now.

"Hey, Alison. How's school?"

The teen just shrugged. "It's school," she said. The attitude she used to dish out had been tempered somewhat. "Come on, squirt." She held her hand out to Eva.

Eva skipped over to Alison and took her hand as if she were her big sister. Eva idolized her, and Karen was sure Alison saw her as the baby sister she'd never had but always wanted.

"I take it everyone's here?" Karen said.

"Yeah," Alison said. "Dad said you had news to share with all of us."

Karen forced herself to keep a straight face, knowing Owen had told everyone she had an announcement just so she wouldn't chicken out. Nothing like being put in the hot seat. She shrugged, then realized Alison was now calling Ryan her dad. Wow, things really had improved in their relationship.

"It appears so," she said. "I take it everyone is waiting to hear from me?" She stepped down into the living room, very aware that Luke hadn't pulled his gaze from her. He was tracking her, just something else he did. His feet were bare, and he had that really intense way of looking at her. She wondered what he was seeing. It was unnerving.

"So what's going on?" Luke was holding a beer bottle, pulling at the label.

Suzanne was now coming her way, carrying a beer, as well, and a glass of white wine. "For you, my dear," she said, her tone amused.

Karen took the wine as everyone made their way into the living room, Marcus and Charlotte, Ryan and Jenny, Owen and their mom. Alison was already sitting on the huge square ottoman across from Luke, with Eva perched on her lap. Karen took a big swallow of her wine.

"So what's going on?" Iris, her mom, said. "Owen said you had something to share with us. Good news, bad news…?" She was still smiling, which was good, as it meant she didn't have a clue what Karen was about to tell her.

Karen couldn't look at Suzanne, who had a big grin. Marcus was standing off to the side, but he wasn't smiling, and neither was Owen. Ryan, she realized, was watching his older brothers, his gaze narrowed as if he'd figured out they knew something. The seconds ticked by in silence.

"Well, do you all remember when I went to law school in Missoula, like my last year there?" Karen said. "I met a guy. His name was Jack Curtis. Long story short, I fell for him. Then came spring break. Remember when I didn't come back to Livingston and drove out east, through Georgia, rural Georgia?" She didn't know why she felt the need to accentuate that point. "We did something really stupid —like, we got married. He was talking it up because of how hot we were for each other, so I said yeah, why not? Then we were standing in front of a backwoods justice of the peace, saying I do. Two days later, we were back in Missoula.

"I walked through the door, so excited because I'd landed this job clerking for Judge Thompson, moving my things in because we were married, so goodbye dorms, and I found him just packing up all his things. He lifted this big suitcase of clothes, told me it was over, we were over, that he'd made a mistake marrying me. The way he looked at me, it was like he hated me. He told me not to call him, that he never wanted to hear from me again… I said a lot of really bad words."

Karen took in Eva's big eyes. Alison, meanwhile, was watching her as if she were the coolest aunt ever. She noted that everyone else was staring at her as if she'd lost her mind. Ryan and Marcus both shot Alison a look, but it was Marcus who said, "Alison, you and Eva, outside, back yard."

She expected an argument from Alison, so she lifted her glass of wine and took another swallow, but the kids left, and she waited until she heard the click of the back door screen. "Anyway, long story short…"

"Don't forget the restraining order," Owen said, jumping in.

Marcus just shook his head and closed his eyes for a second, touching his face. She didn't let herself look at anyone else for too long, because the shock staring back was something she didn't want to see. Then there was Luke, who was looking at her so hard that she could feel his scrutiny.

"Right, there is that," she said. "Yes, apparently I didn't handle it well. I called him over and over, like, two hundred or more times, saying some really bad things and demanding he call me back. But he never did, instead letting every one of my calls go to voicemail. Of course, I was angry, furious, because who does that, marries you and then walks out without a reason, without a discussion? I'm pretty sure I threatened him in every way imaginable, saying his life wasn't worth shit, and I wanted to track him down and kill him. I likely even described in detail how it could happen.

"Next thing I knew, I was served a restraining order, and Sheriff Bert paid me a visit, which was beyond humiliating. Basically, he told me to forget about Jack and move on with my life, because if I picked up the phone and called him again, or tried to locate him, I could find myself in serious trouble. I was to consider the restraining order a form of divine intervention to help me, save me. But Jack had changed his number, anyway. I didn't think there was a reason to tell the sheriff that, because what was the point? So I agreed, said I'd behave myself, swallowed my heart, my pride, and he promised not to tell Marcus, who'd just started working as a deputy.

"At the time, it couldn't have been much worse for me, right? Well, in case you hadn't figured it out, I planned to take this to my grave—except my nosy big brother just happened to show up last night when Jack called. He's found himself in a world of trouble, arrested and in jail, and he called me and—"

"So he wants your help?" Ryan cut in.

She wished everyone would just let her finish. She lifted the glass of wine and took another really big swallow, feeling the buzz. "It seems so," she replied, thinking about the file she'd only started sorting through, the notes and photos of Bonnie, her things, and a catalogue of men's clothes and personal items that had also been found there.

"And you told him to go fuck himself, right?" Luke jumped in, more of a demand than a question.

"Not in so many words..." She looked down at Luke,

seeing the flicker of fire in his blue eyes. If Jack wasn't locked up behind bars, she figured Luke would hunt him down and pay him a visit.

Everyone started talking all at once.

"Hey, hey, hey," Karen said. "Seriously! Look, I saw him and told him I'll help him in arraignment, help him get bail, and then that's it. He has to find himself another lawyer after that. So, if you don't mind, I would like to move past this. Now you know my deepest, most embarrassing secret. It's in the past, and just so we're clear, if you have any questions, ask them now. This is your one and only shot. Then I never want to hear about it again. You'll never get the chance to mention it, throw it in my face, remind me of a time in my life I would like to forget forever."

She took in her family, feeling so much in the spotlight. Generally, that was something she didn't shy away from, but right now, she'd have given anything to slip into the background.

"Yeah, well, you can hold that thought," Marcus said, "because you and I need to have a discussion about the murder charges against him, the crime scene."

She only nodded. Everything in his expression reminded her of the brother she'd once butted heads with.

"Well, I honestly didn't see that coming," their mom said, jumping in. "You kept him a secret all these years? You should have said something. I guess the good thing is that you're divorced. I can understand why you didn't want anyone to know."

"You seriously threatened him?" Ryan added. "Holy shit, and he has a restraining order against you, yet he suddenly has the balls to call you as if you owe him something?"

Karen lifted her glass, knowing Suzanne was frowning,

watching her, because there was so much they didn't know. She took another swallow of the white Chablis. Although she'd suggested questions, she really hadn't intended to answer them.

"You know," Luke said, "what I want to know is if you didn't hear from him again, how did you sign the divorce papers?"

Karen closed her eyes, feeling her brother watching her. *Leave it to Luke…*

"Karen, you did divorce him, right?" Suzanne said.

As she swirled the wine in her glass and lifted it to down the rest, she was glad for the fact that Owen had had the foresight to offer to drive. She had to dig deep for courage as she looked over to Luke, who was still leaning forward, his forearms on his knees, dangling his beer. He'd figured out the one thing she'd told no one.

"Unfortunately, when I said I never heard from him again, I meant it. We are very much still married."

CHAPTER
Seven

KAREN RAN her hands over her face, feeling gritty. Her stomach growled from yet another missed dinner as she listened to the echoing clang of metal and footsteps on concrete. As the heavy steel door opened, she took in the gray walls around her, seeing marks and dirt and spots she'd never noticed before.

"Thanks, Hank," Marcus said to the deputy who had brought Jack in and uncuffed him. Marcus stayed just off to the side, wearing blue jeans, but with his sheriff's badge pinned to his navy T-shirt. His arms were crossed as he surveyed the stranger she'd married.

She had no idea what to say, definitely a first for her, so she simply said, "Jack, this is my brother Marcus," and gestured toward him, though she stayed where she was across the room.

The door closed, and Jack seemed to hesitate as he took in the scene, as if this were a polite society gathering. For a minute, she thought he was going to offer Marcus his hand to shake.

Marcus nodded to him, his arms crossed. "I under-stand you and my sister are still married."

So he was getting straight to the point of the freak-out that had made him park her ass in his cruiser and drive all the way out to Sweetwater County jail. Maybe that was better than her trying to explain to everyone how she could still be married to a man who'd basically told her to get lost.

Karen wasn't sure what to make of Jack's expression, but he didn't pull his gaze from Marcus. "My brother, the sheriff, gave me your file," she said. "After reading it, Jack, I'd say it doesn't look good. There were men's belongings in the hotel room—toiletries, clothes, and receipts with your name on them. You say they weren't yours, or they were planted?" She gestured to the file on the table, which she'd picked up from home after insisting Marcus stop for it. "Open it," she said. "It's all there. You're a lawyer, so take a look. Are those your things? Bonnie wasn't alone. It appears like a quarrel gone wrong."

She could feel her brother staring her down, likely because she wasn't addressing the fact that she and Jack were still married. That was the last thing she wanted to talk about with her brother there.

Jack dragged his gaze from her brother to her and then took a step to the table and opened the file. He winced as he fanned out the photos, looked at the reports. Karen knew her brother was watching her. She wished he wouldn't stay, but she'd never seen him stand his ground the way he was now around Jack.

"I agree," Jack said. "I wouldn't be here now if it looked good. Bonnie, though…she didn't deserve this. From the photos, yes, those are my things, but not things I would have missed, so that tells me someone got into my house, took them, and planted them." He tossed everything back on the table. "Honestly, looking at this, if I were my client, I'd be thinking I'd done it and was lying—but I'm not lying. It's almost perfect."

"Except why would someone want to plant evidence against you?" Marcus asked. If her client had been anyone else, she'd have kicked her brother out. Lawyer–client privilege and all, but this was too personal. This was different.

Jack didn't say anything for a second. When he did, he looked right at Karen. "Because that's the kind of thing that happens when I don't do as I'm told, sticking my nose into things I've been warned away from. Karen, can we have a minute alone?"

Marcus seemed immovable and shook his head. "No, I'm not leaving. You call my sister to come and help you out, yet you filed a restraining order against her after walking out on her after a sham marriage. Now, after how many years of fucking around, you want to have a minute? Well, you won't get one. You think she's supposed to, what, just drop everything for you? No, she's not talking with you alone, and you're not messing with her again. I don't know what kind of games you're playing, but you're done. Since my sister doesn't want to talk about the fact that you're still married, I'll do the talking. You wanted her out of your life, so she's out, and you're going to end this marriage. Karen, file for divorce. Draw up the papers."

She found herself taking in her pumps, which added four inches to her short stature, wondering where her voice had disappeared to.

"And you will sign them," Marcus continued, "and then you'll leave my sister be."

"I can't do that," Jack snapped. "You don't understand. Everything I did was because it was the only way I could protect her."

Karen found herself staring at him. "What are you talking about?"

"Protect her from what?" Marcus cut in.

Jack didn't pull his gaze from her. "Karen…" he started, then let out a sigh, running his hand over the back of his head, maybe because he had finally figured out that her brother wasn't leaving.

"You know what, Jack?" Karen said. "I never expected to see or hear from you again. My brother is right. I'll draw up the divorce papers, and you'll sign them and end something that should have been ended years ago. I honestly don't know about getting you out of jail. That case…you see the file, the photos. You're saying it wasn't you, that someone planted evidence. Why? Now you're even suggesting you were protecting me—from what, from whom?

"I will never forget the way you looked at me as you walked out that door, the way you cut me off. I begged like a fool, but you were so final. It was over. You hated me, and for the life of me, I had no idea what I had done. Of course I acted badly, but what do you expect? You married me, and two days later you were walking out without an explanation. You cut me off completely. If you had sat me down and said, 'Hey, sorry, Karen, but I made a mistake, jumping the gun and marrying you. I was wrong,' I would have been furious, but it would have been better than you blowing me off like you did.

"You never answered one of my calls, not one—and then serving me with a restraining order? Like, who does that? It's not the kind of thing you get over. I still have it, you know, and it's still very much in force, yet here I am, standing here like a fool." She gestured wide and took a step on the concrete, hearing the click of her heel, still in her skirt and blouse, feeling grungy and sweaty and wanting a shower.

He looked away as if considering something, then fanned out the photos on the table, tossing the one of Bonnie over to where her brother lingered. "You're a cop," he said. "What does that look like to you?"

Marcus walked over, lifted the photo, and really looked at it. He dragged his gaze over to Karen, then back to the photo, his hand on his duty belt. "She didn't see it coming," he said. "Bullet to the back of the head, professional."

"A professional, or a hit?" Jack sounded rather calm. "She's down on her knees, maybe, with a gun to the back of her head. What did the coroner's report say? Shot from close range. But why was she there at all? Her cell phone, was it in the list of evidence?" He was looking at Karen, but she watched as Marcus reached for the file. She already knew the answer.

"No cell phone was listed among the items recovered at the scene," she said.

Marcus said nothing as he read, then lifted his blue eyes to her. She could see his question. At the same time, she knew he didn't want her there.

"She never went anywhere without her phone," Jack said. "I told you she called me. Her phone would've shown that, the time. I was at home. From the time frame and when she was shot, there's no way I could have been there, but you'll likely find my DNA all over the room. Meanwhile, I'm sitting here in this cell, trying to piece together why. Now this, seeing these photos…I already know why."

Marcus was a few inches taller than Jack, but the two were about the same build. He took a step closer to him. "You know why? Well, come on, tell us. The suspense is killing me." Sarcasm dripped from his voice.

Karen had to clear her throat, as that knot had once again settled in her stomach.

"We all have secrets somewhere," Jack said. "I never allowed myself to get close to another woman. Bonnie was important to me, but apparently I got careless, just like I did with you. You were a ray of light, but I soon learned I couldn't have that." Jack was looking right at her. Karen didn't want to hear this. A shiver slid up her spine. She had to fight the urge to rub her arms.

"That, there…" Jack gestured to the photo Marcus was holding. "That would have been you, Karen, if I had stayed. That restraining order was for your protection, not mine."

Marcus darted his gaze over to her and then back to Jack. From the way he stiffened, she wondered if he understood that Jack had just yanked the rug out from under her again.

"Excuse me?" Her voice squeaked. "What the hell are you talking about?"

Jack met her stare with his icy blue eyes as he took a step toward her. "You think I wanted to leave you? I really did love you, but I didn't have a choice. I never expected you to fight the way you did. If it had been any other time…" He shook his head, sounding so angry.

Marcus stared him down but said nothing.

"You're telling me the only reason you walked out the door was so I wouldn't end up with a bullet in my head?" Karen took another step, her legs trembling. "What kind of crazy, sick joke is this?"

"So you know who killed this woman," Marcus finally said. "Who? Is my sister in danger? What are you involved in?" He didn't yell, but he did have a way of speaking with such authority that no one was foolish enough to cross him. Even she could feel the subtle bite in his tone.

Jack pulled a hand over his face. He looked so tired, and when he glanced at her, it was with an expression she didn't want to see. "I don't know who pulled the trigger, but at the same time—"

It happened so fast. Marcus pulled his fist back and hit Jack, a punch to his face. He went down with a crash against the table.

"Marcus, what is wrong with you?" Karen yelled as she ran in between them, standing in front of her brother, her hands on his chest as if she could hold him back and stem his anger toward a man she had loved so deeply. She turned to Jack, who had stepped back, blood dripping from the side of his mouth. She felt helpless, horrified, speechless, looking down at a man she'd loved and hated for so long, but she was seeing him now in a way she couldn't make sense of, and all she could do was think, who was Jack Curtis?

KAREN RAN her hand over the back of her neck, flicking her long hair, pacing around the table as Jack stood off to the side, pressing a napkin to his bleeding lip, tracking her every step. It was the quiet that unnerved her. She took in the closed steel door her brother was now on the other side of, speaking with a deputy who was likely filling him in on how hitting a prisoner wasn't allowed, or something along those lines.

"Well, I guess I had that coming," Jack said rather calmly. Blood had dripped onto his wrinkled white shirt.

She pulled her arms across her chest as she faced him, trying to make sense of everything he'd said. "Yeah, well, what can I say? My family's not handling this too well, considering I never told them I married you. You're right, though: You had it coming. You won't make trouble for my brother, will you? Like ask them to press charges?" She held her breath for a second, having never seen Marcus lose it like that. She wasn't sure what to make of the way Jack watched her as he pulled back the chair and sat down. His lip was swelling but no longer bleeding.

"No, of course not," he said. "I can understand why he did it. So you never told them about us?"

She exhaled, her arms still crossed. "I never planned on telling them, considering everything that happened—but you showing up, calling me, you kind of created a situation, and I had to tell my family tonight."

"Right, you have a big family. How many brothers, again?" From the way he looked up at her, she thought he was trying to add a bit of lightness to a situation where there wasn't any.

"Four, and a sister. So who is it, Jack?" she said. She didn't miss his confusion. "You didn't answer my question before my brother settled his fist in your face." She knelt down to the photos splayed all over the floor and picked them up one by one.

He was there beside her, reaching for them and taking them from her. It was the image of Bonnie and what was left of her head that he took from her first.

"Are you telling me you left me all those years ago so I wouldn't end up shot, killed, like her?" Karen said. "I don't understand, Jack. That makes no sense at all. Then you said the restraining order was to protect me. Come on, Jack. I don't like games. What's really going on?"

He picked up the file, as well, which had gone flying during her brother's outburst. She was glad she had a moment alone with Jack. "Yes, Karen, I left because I allowed myself to fall in love with you. Marrying you was my mistake, because you weren't a secret anymore. You know, as a lawyer, I can see the beauty in a well-told lie. You can manipulate the truth, control the story—but the minute I put the ring on your finger, I lost all control. I had to create a story when I realized my mistake and the danger I put you in."

"What the…?" She knew she'd stuttered. She was flustered.

He let out a heavy sigh.

She moved away from him, mainly because she didn't know what the hell to do. "I think you need to start at the beginning, Jack. This doesn't make sense. Are you in trouble, or were you? Why would someone want to hurt me because I married you? That's ridiculous. Are you telling me that Bonnie is dead because—"

"I allowed myself to care again." He cut her off. "Yes, she is very much dead because I didn't keep her at arm's length, didn't control her. Because I can't be controlled. You know, it was fine, the affair, the meaningless sex, the dating, nothing serious. But the minute I cared, the minute I shared things about my family… They're crazy, dangerous. Yeah, that would have been you. That was why I walked out the door when I knew what was going to happen. I'd grown careless, believing I could just move away and start my own life. I had to, Karen." He put the file on the table and started toward her, to touch her, she thought, so she shrugged and stepped away.

"What the fuck? This is crazy. What kind of family do you have that they would do that? That's ludicrous. It makes absolutely no sense." She knew she was yelling. She didn't want him to touch her, and she lifted her hands for him to back off when he went to reach for her again. This time, he stepped back as if he realized what he was doing wasn't helping.

"I know it sounds crazy," he said. "I don't know what I was thinking when I met you other than just maybe, I could be happy—as if I had a right to be happy. I tried to tell myself that marrying you was a crazy instant reaction, but I just knew I wanted everything with you. I was thinking how simple our life could be. Then, just as fast, everything came crashing down. I was happy for a moment, thinking maybe I could have a future like everyone else. I hadn't given a second thought to my family, how they work. They wouldn't just let us be, because they'd use you to keep me in line.

"I'd heard it from my father, growing up, that we weren't like everyone else. I couldn't have you anywhere near them, so I did the only thing I could think of. I walked away from you, told them you were a mistake, meaningless. I knew everything I said had to be damn convincing or they'd never believe me, so I played your messages, every one of them. It just about killed me, hearing the hurt, the anger, knowing I deserved all of it and more. You said just enough that I could do something to ensure you never came near me…" He pressed his hands to the back of the metal chair, squeezing the frame as he leaned down.

Her chest tightened, and she struggled to breathe. "Why…?" Her throat ached. Everything ached. She wanted to step back, but she couldn't get her feet to move.

"Because I was selfish. I just wanted to be happy, but I knew that wouldn't happen. I was selfish for bringing you in, for letting you believe we could have a future." He was shaking his head.

She couldn't wrap her head around what he was saying. "I don't get it. Why would you want me to stay away from your family? Who are they? This is starting to sound like the mob or something. They wouldn't like me, or they…what? What do you mean, they would use me against you?" she yelled, gesturing toward him.

"Oh, they would've liked you. You're perfect. They'd have seen how much I loved you. You're the perfect person to keep me in line. But I'm not made like they are. I would've had to sell my soul so nothing would happen to you or your family." He stood up, rested his hands on his hips, and took a step toward her. "Maybe you do need to understand who they are, what they are. The family I was born into isn't anything like yours. They're not regular folks who work for the simple things in life. They plan everything, and I mean everything, over decades and lifetimes. They don't feel the kind of remorse you do or differentiate between right and wrong.

"I went to law school for them. They planned it out for me. I was supposed to go to Yale, their pick, but I went against everything and landed at Missoula. I mean, how could I have done that, changed the rules, the script? With their connections to Yale, I would've been invited easily, unlike the average person. But I know too much, and they've never been able to control me and make me do what I was supposed to. I had the one thing my father, his brothers, and all of them didn't: a sense of right and wrong, a conscience. To them, that was nothing but weakness." The way he was looking at her, she'd never seen that kind of intensity, and for a moment, it reminded her of when he'd left.

"You keep saying 'they.' Who are you talking about, your family?"

He was looking at her as if deciding what to share. "You know anything about secret societies?"

She said nothing, only lifted her hand and glanced to the door again before flicking her gaze back to him. "Likely not enough, only in passing."

He nodded. "Well, that's good for your safety. It's not as if they advertise. Only the upper echelons of society are part of those kinds of groups, the families who make things happen. When you think of the mob, you're right in a sense, except these are families whose names you've never heard. You don't know who they are because they keep it that way. You won't find anything about them on the internet, in books…"

Her heart thudded. She wished Marcus would come back in right about then.

"And when I say 'they,' I don't mean just my father and other distant family members. There are other families like them, and they do business with each other, entertain with each other, live their lives only with each other. They never marry outside that group, because to bring in an outsider is never allowed. As for me, who they can't control, I'm kind of like a loose thread. I've never proved my loyalty, and that makes anyone close to me a target."

"So it's not the mob?"

Was he about to laugh? He made a sound, then shook his head. "In a way, yes, but I'm talking the orders and secret groups that run everything. You wouldn't have any idea, because they know how to stay hidden. You may have heard the Trilateral Commission and Bilderberg meetings mentioned briefly, invite only, attended by the most powerful in the world, including kings and leaders. The Council on Foreign Relations, Skull and Bones…those are just a few with a public face and diverse membership. Truly secret societies are controlled by a handful at the top, and no one really knows what goes on aside from manipu-lation. How many are there?" He gestured to her. "Karen, I want you to think about orders like the Freemasons and the non-profits tied to them. To be clear, the lower eche-lons have no fucking idea what the top creeps are doing and how they're being manipulated into doing their bidding. They don't even know who the real leaders are.

"Think of every public policy and how it came about. They know how to stay hidden. On the internet, you may hear names whispered, but that's all you'll hear. Membership is for the notable only. The truth is something you can find only outside of the classroom, outside the walls of universities, outside boardrooms. No one really knows all the details. There are more than a few men in suits talking about power and money, and every one of those guys knows how to shut it down and spin questions to make it seem like the people asking are crazy or spewing nonsense, playing up a conspiracy.

"They can easily have you labeled delusional, a conspiracy nutcase, and tossed in jail or suddenly under investigation by the feds. They own every politician, and they don't start at the top but at the bottom, infiltrating only the key areas they need. Think school boards, city councilors, mayors, sheriffs, congressmen, lawyers, judges. Then there are the illegally funded three-letter agencies many have never heard of… Shall I keep going?"

Karen just looked at him. What kind of bullshit story was this, anyway? Maybe her expression said what she was thinking.

"Look, Karen, if you want the truth, I'll tell you, but the reality is that you can't handle it. Everything they do is planned. Any proof that exists is destroyed. They're the ones who craft bills and laws with legal bullshit the average person never reads. Before the internet existed, they burned unwanted documents or scratched out names and references from records. They control the internet, the banks, and every seat of power from Wall Street board-rooms to the corridors of government. They have existed for centuries behind the scenes, a mysterious influence on the world that you can't even imagine."

What was it about the way he spoke? It had always riveted her, but right now, as she allowed herself to take in their surroundings, she couldn't get her head around what he was saying. "You're right," she said. "You sound delu-sional. For a minute there, I almost believed you. It's a great story and almost makes what you did sound reasonable, except the world doesn't work that way."

"You sure about that, Karen? The society my family is a part of, its members are prominent. They've already ensured that the next sitting judge of the second circuit will be their person, and they control the industries, the agencies that run our cities and countries. How do you think they can get away with the kinds of things they do? You know about the shadowy side of life that no one else does, the deep state. Everyone is handpicked. The society is steeped so deep in racism, bigotry, and elitism. They excluded women until recently, too. They're responsible for things the world over that no one would ever believe, and the only way they survive is on the misery of others."

She just stared at him. "So your family is…"

"Not just wealthy, no," he said. "Growing up, I didn't really know. I saw and heard the kinds of things your average kid never would, closed-door meetings with powerful people who made things happen. I remember being called in by my dad one day. I was back from school. That was my first time hearing about reprisals. I was told to just fall in line, because when I didn't listen to a request, which was really an order, there would be punishment. They could destroy people. They had a way of controlling us. You didn't talk, because if you did, they knew where you banked—and that was just what they did to the little guy, your average peon out there.

"I learned early on that they had members on the councils of all the major banks. They'd ensure you never got credit again. Their members were influential people in influential positions. You already know that the CIA is known for its shadowy acts, pulling the strings from positions of power, so how many of the society are in there, running things from within US intelligence agencies? They definitely don't like people tampering and prying into what they do. Think about it, Karen. How many suicides are really cases of someone knowing too much? Sometimes someone suddenly grows a conscience and does something really stupid, like trying to become a whistleblower. In one case, the corrupt attorney general that would-be whistleblower divulged to was on our payroll, and the testimony disappeared. So did the person who believed in right and wrong.

"One family launched the international drug trade, putting heroin onto the streets, and they still maintain it today from their positions in government. Controlling the drug trade is a huge step toward gaining financial power. So is trafficking, human trafficking. They control the illusion of choice, playing the public like puppets. They own properties, islands. This super elite group has a history that goes back hundreds of years. But you're likely thinking, so what?"

She just stared at Jack. She couldn't get her tongue to move because she didn't know what to say.

"I can see you don't get it—or maybe you do," he said. "My father was picked. My uncle was picked. I was picked, but I said no, because I understood clearly that this group has their hands in every level of power in this country. Did I see and hear the backroom deals?" He shook his head. "No one in the outside world has any idea of the kinds of things they can do. You understand? They're in government, industry, media, finance. They run not just this country but the world. They own the news networks people believe are telling them the truth. They control what you watch on TV. What you're told is what this group wants and needs you to know. I had my own plans, to run for the DA's office, then attorney general, senator, governor, the White House. All of it, but the right way. They could have made it happen, would have made it happen…but I wasn't joining them, not with how they did things. I knew how they operated, and maybe I was naive, believing I could step away from them and be a good guy.

"One time, I was at the drycleaner's with my mom. I wasn't even that old, just a little kid. This guy my mom knew—let's call him Charles—he walks in, friendly as all hell, like a gentleman. I remember his reaction to a stain on his shirt that hadn't come out. Like, who cares, right? Buy another damn shirt. He was a wealthy man. Well, he went on about it with the drycleaner, calling him out. The owner stood up to him, arguing that it was a blood stain and wouldn't come out, and I remember Charles said he'd make sure the owner didn't get the opportunity to ruin another man's shirt. Like, was he kidding?

"Next thing I knew, a few days later, maybe a week, the man was out of business, gone. His place was bulldozed down, and my father and uncle were joking about the bloodstained shirt, and the lesson the drycleaner would learn for speaking back the way he had. Charles had just made a call. It was nothing for him, but he had taken everything from that man. I didn't know him, but I was old enough to understand that kind of thing wasn't going to be part of who I was. It sickened me, hearing it. I said no when Yale called to say I was in. I applied to Missoula instead. Did my family let me go happily? No, but they did let me go. I thought it was easy. Great, I was out from under their thumb.

"But they knew everything I was doing. The minute I married you, they knew. The day we got back from Georgia, it was the happiest and worst day of my life. You'd gone to pick up your things. It wasn't my dad who called; it was my uncle at the door, with his associate. I recognized him, the guy who did the dirty work when my dad needed something cleaned up, someone disappeared, someone taken care of. They knew about you, your family, your mother… I just had to come back into the family, and everything would be fine. That was what men did, he pointed out to me. We run things, decide things, change things. I'd run the country one day—but not really, because it would be them behind the scenes, really running things, telling me what to do, what to say, and giving me speeches to read. I said I was happy, that I wanted a simple life and to do things the right way, my way…and you know what my uncle said?"

Why was he telling her this now? She was being flung back into that memory, not wanting to relive that feeling, that ache, even though it was burned into her. She knew it had happened a certain way, the way he'd looked at her, talked to her, gutted her. Now he was trying to say it had been a lie. She fisted her hands and pulled her arms around her middle again, crossing them tight because that was the only way she could keep it together.

"I can see you're having a hard time with this," Jack said.

"You're kidding, right? Eight years is a long time, and everything in this story, Jack, is…" She lifted her hands in the air. Damn, her thoughts were spinning.

"Unbelievable, I know. But you need to understand, Karen, I was young and idealistic, and I'd just had the rug yanked out from under me, knowing they wanted to bring me in as a young man and groom me, train me, condition me to be placed in a position of power and carry out the agenda of the older members. They don't operate in isolation. They're just a thread in a greater web, producing the leaders and stewards of the ruling class, diplomats, spies, senators, Supreme Court justices. They basically funnel who they want into positions of power and influence. They form companies whose investors are family, society members. It's not just an old boys' network. It's a vicious group of interbred bloodlines seeking to impose their will and their way of life upon the global population, pillaging, stealing, enslaving. If people really understood their secrets, they'd understand they live in anything but the land of the free.

"My uncle's associate said it was funny: One of your brothers could suddenly find himself under investigation. And he knew every one of them, Marcus, Luke, Ryan, Owen. A murder charge was always good, especially when the weapon's found on the suspect. It would have been planted in a car or a house, hidden in a closet. Drugs were another option, considering your brothers' pasts. Or maybe your mom would have an accident. I knew the minute he said it that I was being cornered, and I couldn't have that. I loved you. I knew they'd find a way to use you against me, so I did the only thing I knew I could do. I would rather you hate me than see you hurt.

"Recently, a case landed on my desk, a complaint of insider trading against a senator on their payroll. I refused to make it go away. Can I prove it was them who shot Bonnie after I was warned to drop the case?" He shook his head. "No, you'll never prove it. They're too good, too powerful, exerting too much influence. Any evidence would've been planted professionally, but my credibility is now destroyed, and the new media gaslighting will be the final nail in my coffin. The local authorities here wouldn't have just stumbled upon it."

She pressed her hands to her face just as the door opened and Marcus stepped in with the deputy. She was absolutely gutted. "I don't understand. Why Bonnie? This doesn't make any sense…"

The deputy cuffed Jack again, and she wanted to yell

for him to stop. She strode over, right over to Jack, and touched his arm. Something in his eyes had her freaking out, shaking. Like, who the hell were these people? Who the hell was Jack, really?

"Because Bonnie knew about the case and my family. She was in the next room when I was paid a visit and told to make the case go away," he said. "She was furious. She talked about exposing them. I heard my uncle say once that if the American people really knew what our family had done, they'd chase us down the street with torches and pitchforks and lynch us. Bonnie didn't understand that no one talks and lives. You'd think someone would talk, but no one does, not ever, because everyone is subject to blackmail. Everyone has secrets. Loose ends aren't something they have.

"Bonnie wasn't just a friend; she was a reporter, and she likely talked to the wrong person, trusted the wrong person. Now, because they can't control me, can't get me to bow to them, I too am a threat. Killing me would be easy, but the best way to silence me is with a murder charge, by killing someone close to me, someone I care about. Not only have they destroyed my credibility, but now they've ensured no one will want to listen to me. So when I say the evidence was planted and I didn't do this, I'm telling you the truth."

THIS WAS BIGGER THAN HER.

Listening to Jack and the nonsense he'd spewed had her thinking he was insane. What he'd shared had sounded crazy, like a villain talking about global domination and running the world. That was all she could think of. She had to dial him back. This was not the kind of thing to base a defense on. At the same time, something about his paranoia had planted a seed of doubt in her.

"You haven't said two words since we left," Marcus said.

She took in the file in her lap, glad her brother was driving. It was dark, and she was hungry, but she didn't think she could eat. "What do you want me to say, that he's evidently crazy? You want me to also point out that you shouldn't have hit him? That was really stupid on your part. I have to figure out a defense by Monday based on some conspiracy I have no proof of. Sure, if I had an army of investigators, years to prepare, and an unlimited budget, maybe I could suggest there's some truth to what he's saying, even though you and I both know it's impossible. It's not believable."

"Not really," Marcus replied. "But I don't think you should stay at your place alone tonight. In fact, I don't want you alone at all right now."

Karen turned to her brother, resting her hands over the file. She'd decided not to open it again, because after hearing Jack's explanation, she couldn't shake the image of the dead woman, a bullet to the back of her head. Could that really have been her instead?

She was about to say no, she wanted to go home, but something about all of this had left her so unsettled. "Maybe you're right. Sounds like you believe him. I know you were out there, listening to everything, but it's crazy, Marcus."

"Yeah, what exactly do you know about this man, Karen? I mean really, and no bullshit answers. What do you know about his family, where he's from?"

Something about the way he asked had her racking her brain. "Evidently not very much, because everything he said tonight flies in the face of what I believed. I thought he just didn't like his family, that they were pushy, wanted him to be something he wasn't prepared for. They had their ideas, and he had his. That was all he ever said." She let out a breath. "I don't know. If I think back now, is there anything that makes sense in what he's saying? It's crazy talk," she added, more to convince herself.

"You sure about that? I don't have my head buried in the sand. It may not be as crazy as it sounds. Karen, if it is true, I don't want you anywhere near him. He shouldn't have called you. He should just leave you be, because if he has family with that kind of power… I'm not saying I believe his story, but there are some really bad people out there, and they do things even I can't explain." Marcus was shaking his head. From the way he dragged his hand over his face, he needed a shave. She knew he was worried.

"Can you do something for me?" she said.

"Depends. What is it?" He sounded pissed and tired, too.

"Can you run a background check on Jack? Find everything you can. Red flags, anything. At least rule out a mental health problem, psychosis, before we tread anywhere near this rabbit hole of secret societies and men trying to run his life. I would really like to have my career as a lawyer continue, and I need to know what I'm dealing with before I talk to the DA or we go before the judge."

"I already plan on dissecting every part of his life, but thanks for asking for my help," he said. He was teasing, she thought, even though everything about this seemed so dire.

"You know what?" she said. "I think I'm going to talk to Luke, pick his brain from a military perspective. I think maybe I'll crash at Mom's tonight, too."

He let out a breath. "Yeah, I think that's an even better idea."

SHE WATCHED as Marcus carried a sleeping Eva to the car and tucked her in the back seat. Alison followed and slid in beside her, and Charlotte brought up the rear. Ryan and Jenny were now long gone, Suzanne had been called in to the fire station, and she had no idea where Owen had disappeared, as his plumbing van was gone. Karen stood at her mom's living room window, hearing her mom doing dishes or something in the kitchen. She shoved the last bite of the chicken sandwich her mom had made her in her mouth.

"So are you going to tell me what's going on, or are

you going to stand there all night and stare out the window?" Luke lifted the bowl of potato chips beside him, but she only waved it off.

A soccer game was on TV, and the noise was welcome. Who was playing, she didn't have a clue. She hadn't known her brother watched soccer. She took in the four empty beers on the sofa table in front of him.

"Jack said some things tonight that kind of freaked me out a bit," Karen said, taking in the way Luke was peeling off the label of one of the bottles.

Luke dragged his gaze from the beer bottle to the kitchen and then back to her. The way his gaze deepened, she wondered if he already knew. "Marcus filled me in some when you were talking to Mom after getting back. You know, Karen, you can either make it difficult or not. But my advice is to get your divorce, quick and quiet. C'est la vie, baby. This isn't the kind of trouble you want in your back yard or the kind of people you want in your life. You're not equipped to handle them. Tell him to get another lawyer, and you cut ties and never talk to him or see him again."

She pulled at her mom's sweater, which she'd helped herself to, feeling the chill even though the house was warm. She'd have to grab a pair of sweats, too, something she'd done more than a time or two when staying over. "If it's true, if he did all this to protect me…"

"So what, Karen?" Luke snapped, setting the bottle down with a clank on the table and looking up at her. "There's a lot of shit out there you're not equipped to handle. Stay out of it, stay away from it. This was how many years ago? If this is who he is, then I don't want you mixed up in this with him. If it's true, he did the right thing, so you do the right thing, too, and walk away. There's no happy ending here for you. He did you a favor.

Let's just hope, if it's true, that he hasn't suddenly also put you back on their radar—though I guarantee you never left their radar in the first place."

Karen realized their mom had quietly walked into the room with an odd look on her face, one she'd worn too often when she had something on her mind. The room settled into quiet.

"So you're okay with me crashing here tonight, Mom?" Karen said. She didn't know why she felt the need to ask.

"Of course it's okay," Luke said. "Take my room. I'll sleep out here."

Her mom was shaking her head. "You know that's not something you ever have to ask. This is always your home, wherever I am, no matter how old you are, no matter where you live." Her mom didn't look away at first. Then she did, pulling in a heavy breath, lifting her hands in the air. "Look, I know there are likely things going on that you don't want to discuss. At the same time, Karen, you're still married to a man we don't know. We talked about you while you were gone with Marcus to see him. What bothered me was hearing how off the rails you went, and you felt you couldn't tell me, us. I do understand, Karen, more than you think. Just take some time. Stay here awhile so you can figure things out."

For a moment, she wasn't sure what to make of what her mom had said. Iris walked over to her and gave her a hug, something she hadn't done in a long time.

"I'll put out some pajamas and things for you," she said. Then she was gone, and Karen turned to Luke, who still wore that unreadable expression. He reached for the remote and turned the TV off.

"So what was that about?" Karen gestured to where their mom had walked, down the hall to her bedroom.

Luke paused. "You've always had a fiery personality,

Karen. You kind of threw everyone tonight with this secret husband. You've been married to him all these years, and not a word to any of us. You know what else I know? You find trouble and refuse to walk away from it. You confront it head on, damn the consequences. It's noble, but not in this, because I know enough about these kinds of people to know you're way out of your league. I have to wonder why he set his sights on you, Karen. Only a selfish man would put you on the radar of people who can do anything and get away with it."

Luke stood and walked to the window behind her, looked out, and then strode to the front closet to open the lockbox he kept there. He pulled out a gun and checked the rounds before he tucked it in the waistband of his jeans behind him. Something about the sound of metal on metal had the knot twisting in her stomach again. Her hand pressed to her chest, and she suddenly felt a chill in a room that wasn't cold.

"You expecting trouble?" Her voice was strong, but she didn't feel so confident.

"I've seen evils the average person would never be able to wrap their head around. It's who I am. These people are very real, and they can make things happen. I go into the kind of shit I can't talk about, and I deal with people who don't exist, at levels of government where they don't give a shit about you or me, only themselves. I know enough to know that any orders that come down are not for the good of the people, even though me and my team still do our very best out there. Go get some sleep. I'll keep an eye out."

For a second, she didn't know what to say.

Luke rested his hand on her arm. "This is what I do, Karen, and I'm really fucking good at it. Trust me. No one is going to come sneaking around here."

She glanced at the file on the table and nodded, then picked it up. "You know what, Luke? I'm really good at what I do, too. And if any of this is true, then I'm not sure me telling Jack to find someone else to get him out of jail would make a difference. Thanks for the pep talk." She started for the stairs.

"Karen, a word of advice," Luke said.

She turned back to him, seeing the sadness and strength that often lurked in those O'Connell blue eyes. "Sure, why not?"

He didn't smile. "Trust no one, and don't go anywhere alone."

CHAPTER

Ten

AS KAREN WALKED through the door of the jail, she wondered if it was lack of sleep or the fact that Luke was right behind her that had her frazzled and on edge. Her wet hair was pulled back in a ponytail, and she wore sneakers and cream-colored sweatpants. Luke had insisted on practicality in the event they needed to move if something went sideways, which had left Karen a little rattled.

"I'm going in," she said, then turned to Luke, and he only nodded as she gestured to the desk a deputy was approaching.

"I'm here to see Jack Curtis," she said. "I'm his lawyer, Karen O'Connell."

The deputy only nodded before motioning her around the desk, and she glanced back to Luke, who was standing by the door like a pit bull who saw everything.

She was led into the same concrete interrogation room, where she waited, resting her briefcase on the table. She left the file and the notes she'd worked tirelessly on as she strode over to the one-way glass, wondering if someone was there on the other side, watching. She felt as if every-thing she believed had been turned completely upside down.

She heard footsteps, then the steel door. With her arms crossed over her favorite Cubs T-shirt, she took in Jack, who was looking even rougher after another night behind bars. He didn't smell any better, either.

"Well, you could use a shower," she said as the deputy left and the door closed. She noted he wasn't even cuffed this time, and she wondered why.

He settled his hands on his hips and looked at her. "I could use a lot of things, namely getting the hell out of here."

"I'm working on it." She gestured to the table and walked around it.

Jack pulled out a chair on the other side and sat down, taking her in. She wasn't sure what to make of the way he was looking at her, the way he purposely dragged his gaze over her. It was intimate and unsettling. Then an odd smile touched his lips. "You look comfortable," he said. "Casual Sunday? And you look...good. I never told you that."

She paused as she pulled out the file and then sat down, retrieving her legal pad of paper and scribbled notes. "You flirting with me? This is what I wear on the weekends, and Luke, you know, the special forces soldier, seems worried I may have to run."

Jack ran his hands over his face and let out a heavy sigh. "So your brother has an idea of what I've warned you about. I presume you shared everything." He gestured toward her.

"It seemed important, considering the circumstances." She leaned in and wondered if he'd take issue.

"And no, I'm not flirting," he said. "You'd know if I was. I can see how shook up you are. You never were good at hiding how you were feeling. I haven't really asked how you are."

She pressed her hands flat to the file and took in the way he watched her, the way his blue eyes had softened, and the dark whiskers from two days without shaving. She lifted her hands and let them fall with a sigh. "I'm fine. What do you want me to say, Jack? Look, I'm tired. After everything, I feel like you've dragged me over an emotional rollercoaster."

He was leaning forward, his hands together on the table, and for a moment, she thought he'd reach over and touch her. She hoped he wouldn't. She was still trying to understand why she couldn't hate him.

"The truth?" he said. "I know you're angry with me, and you have every right to be, but I never would've called you if I'd thought there was another way. I just want you to be safe, Karen. I didn't ask for this to happen or want it to happen, but it did. I guess, walking out on you, I thought they'd stop. I had to make it look as if I hated you so they couldn't use you against me, because if they hurt you…" He stopped talking and shook his head. Her heart thudded again. "I never stopped thinking about you."

She made herself sit back in the chair. It was hard to look at him, only because it scared the hell out of her, if he was being honest, and that made her angry. "Really, you never stopped thinking about me? So I've been on your mind all these years?"

When his gaze softened again, she could feel herself being sucked back in. "It's kind of what happens when you watch over someone. I checked on you, watched you, knew where you were and when you came back to Livingston to set up your one-woman show over a bar. You've done a lot of good for a lot of people."

She made herself cross her legs because she could feel

them trembling at how twisted this sounded. She leaned forward in the chair, holding her pen and clicking it, taking in everything in front of her. "You were watching me all these years?"

He said nothing for a second, but at least he didn't look away. "Yes."

She nodded and opened the file, then pushed her notes away. She sat back again. "That's so totally fucked up, Jack."

He shrugged. "It is, but I had to be sure nothing happened to you, that you were okay." He quirked the corner of his mouth. "You're still pissed at me, but I can live with that. What I couldn't live with is something happening to you, anyone hurting you."

"Yet you said nothing, and that story last night…"

He reached forward, pressed his hand over hers, and squeezed for a second. "It may sound crazy, but I think you know deep down it's not. My family are the kind of people who fit in with everyone, neighbors, business associates, with the clout to do what they want. Money, position, and power have so many gravitating toward them. After fifteen minutes in a room, you'd think, wow, what a warm and caring person. But I know what they're capable of, and I didn't want you mixed up in it. I was selfish to have married you, but somehow I thought I could have a life away from them with you. What can I say? I've made some bad choices, but out of all those, I wasn't about to do the bidding of those people. I have my own ideals, you know. I need to be able to sleep at night, and stepping on people isn't something I'll do."

She didn't think she could talk about this anymore. "You know my brothers, my family, expect me to draw up divorce papers now. What I don't understand, Jack, is you say you wanted me at arm's length and away from your family, not to be influenced by them or controlled because of what you believed they'd do to me or my family. Yet I had no idea where you were. You disappeared, cut me off. Last night, you tried to explain it away as being for my protection, but the thing is, I'm a big girl. The truth would have been better. I'd have—"

"What?" He cut her off quite sharply. "You'd have what, Karen? Walked away meekly?" He made a rude noise. "There was nothing meek or reasonable about you. You're a tiger, a pit bull. Every one of those messages you left me, I heard your anger, how pissed you were, how hurt you were. I could feel your rage, and it killed me, hearing how much I hurt you. There was no way you would've walked away if I asked you to. You can't hide your feelings. I needed you to hate me, and you did, right?"

She gripped her pen. She didn't know where this put them. Thinking back to who she had been then and who she was now, they were two different people, but that gut punch had scarred her so deeply that every decision she made now was because of what he'd done, what she'd allowed him to do to her.

"Yeah, you gutted me, but you know that already. You never answered me about the divorce. If you really wanted me gone, why did you never send divorce papers?"

He was quiet for a second and lifted his hand, pulling it over his jaw. "Because that would be so final. I had them drawn up and went to send them I don't know how many times, but I couldn't." He let out a rough laugh. "I loved you, and this may sound damn selfish, but if I couldn't have you, I didn't want anyone else to. At least this way, no man could ever marry you."

She tossed the pen on the table and leaned forward,

looking at the door and then back at Jack. "Yet you moved on with another woman. You wanted to, what, keep an eye on me, keep me tied to you? That's sick, Jack…"

"No, it's selfish, Karen, very selfish. I won't apologize for that."

She lifted her hands. "Well, I guess we could agree on that much. It's very selfish, Jack. Look, let's just table this, because we need to talk about a strategy to get you out on bail. Considering what they have here, I wouldn't be getting my hopes up, if I were you, because unless the judge is in a really good mood, I don't know how I'm going to sell bail, even for you. Let me be very clear: I will not bring up or even mention any of the craziness you were talking about last night. Conspiracy…"

"Truth, Karen. It's the truth." Jack cut her off and leaned in.

Karen only shook her head. "Sometimes the truth is what you can't say. It's not believable. I don't plan on working a conspiracy angle, because then I'll become a joke in the legal community. I've worked too damn hard to get where I am, so my plan is to take all that evidence they have and cast a big shadow over it, taking open and shut to anything but."

"And how are you planning on accomplishing that?"

"We need to give them someone else to focus on. You know a good story will beat facts every time. Just one of the things we learned in law school."

He said nothing for a second but seemed to be considering it. "Okay, so what kind of story do you have in mind?"

She reached for her notebook, filled with notes she had scribbled down the night before. "Well, first, tell me what you can about Bonnie—what she did, who she knew, what she was thinking, and exactly what she was investigating. Anything and everything."

Jack paused, then inclined his head, considering. "All right," he said. "Let's get started."

CHAPTER
Eleven

IT WAS twenty past nine on Monday morning when Karen strode across the concrete floor of the courthouse in her four-inch pumps, holding her head high, wearing a navy skirt and blazer with a sleeveless cream blouse underneath, her red hair in a ponytail. She pulled her cell phone from her pocket and silenced it before stuffing it into the side of the briefcase. Her sheriff brother, Marcus, in his uniform shirt and blue jeans, was coming her way.

"Karen." He gestured to her just outside the courtroom doors. "I, uh, did some digging on your husband in there." The way he said it had her stiffening. There was no smile on his face.

"And? Come on, Marcus. I have about two minutes before I have to be in that courtroom. I need you to get right to it." She motioned for him to hurry up as she tried to keep her thoughts centered and focused.

He glanced around and then gestured for her to move to the side. "Jack is a lawyer in Missoula. He worked full time for the DA's office until a week ago. Has no kids—that he knows about, anyway. No criminal charges or even a parking ticket against him. He's clean that way. He doesn't have any outstanding debts, owns a decent-sized house outright, has a sizeable trust he's never used, and drives a Mercedes, a Lincoln, and a Porsche. Apparently, he has a thing for high-end vehicles. He's an only child. His family owns a number of businesses, manufacturing, textiles, investments and such. That's it. No red flags, no priors, nothing in the system that I can find to say he has any kind of mental disorder or anything questionable. But that's only the surface. You know there's a lot more off paper. I could dig only so far, with the little time I had, without setting off flags." His concern stared back at her. Then Marcus flicked his O'Connell blue eyes over her head and past her, and he nodded. "I see Luke is tagging along."

Karen held her briefcase in both hands in front of her as she glanced over her shoulder. Luke was dressed in blue jeans and a faded army T-shirt, lounging off to the side, watching everyone and everything. His shoulder-length dark hair just added to his casual appearance. He was never far away.

"Yeah, he's good to his word, hasn't let me out of his sight, but considering everything, I'm kind of grateful for that. He knows more than me, but he doesn't rub it in, either."

Marcus just nodded, but he didn't smile at the jibe. "Well, he has his way, and we have ours. Watch your back."

She knew he cared. "Listen, thanks for digging. I kind of suspected all that, anyway. I've got to get in there. See you after?"

He started past her, pressing his hand to her shoulder. "Yup, my place. Owen will be there. Suzanne and Ryan will bring the beer."

Then he was gone, and she glanced back to Luke, who jutted his chin toward her. She started to the courtroom and pulled open the door.

When she stepped inside, a few of the seats were taken. She walked right up to the defense table, seeing Tibo Lewis, the DA, in a dark suit and red tie. So she'd gotten the big guns. She hesitated a second when he looked over to her.

"Karen," was all he said.

"Tibo. Didn't know you'd be here," she replied. She retrieved the file from her briefcase and rested it on the table as she pulled out her chair, then set her briefcase on the floor at her feet. She didn't miss his lack of response as she glanced over to him again.

At the back of the room, the door opened. Jack was in the same wrinkled white shirt and tailored pants, his hands cuffed. The sheriff's deputy held his arm, leading him to her, where he was uncuffed and seated at the table.

"You get any sleep?" she said.

He glanced over to her and made a face. "Seriously? Just get me out of here," was all he got out before the bailiff announced, "Presiding Judge Roy Baldwin."

She frowned, taking in the gray-haired man who'd entered. "Okay, this is weird," she said. "I was expecting Judge Thompson."

Jack had showered but still hadn't shaved, appearing much like a man who'd spent two days behind bars. "I don't like this," he said. "Got a bad feeling. What do you know about him?" He narrowed his gaze, staring over at the judge.

Karen rested her hand on his arm. "Nothing. Never seen or heard about him before."

The judge said, "Good morning, everyone. Sit on down. So what do we have here?"

"Your Honor," Tibo said, and buttoned his navy suit jacket as he stood up, "the DA's office received information and new evidence early this morning that Jack Curtis is no longer a suspect in the death of the victim, Bonnie Henderson. The DA's office is withdrawing all criminal charges against Mr. Curtis, as evidence has surfaced regarding a new suspect. From what I understand, a warrant has been issued. We apologize for wasting the court's time and would like to apologize for any inconvenience to Mr. Curtis."

There was a murmur in the courtroom. Karen thought her ears were ringing, and she glanced over to Jack, who was staring at the judge with an odd look. He glanced to her, and she touched his arm, but he only shook his head.

The judge slipped on his glasses as Tibo handed a file to the bailiff, who passed it over to him.

Karen turned to Jack, again leaning close. "You know anything about this?"

He only shook his head again, then glanced behind him and back to the judge. As he sat forward in his chair, by his expression, it seemed he was trying to put together a puzzle. "I do believe I was just sent a message," he said in a low voice, leaning close to her.

The judge banged his gavel. "Very well. This court dismisses all charges against Jack Curtis. Mr. Curtis, you're free to go."

Karen was now standing beside Jack, taking in a judge she'd never seen before, who left the courtroom as quickly as he'd arrived.

"Karen, great to see you," Tibo said as he picked up his briefcase. She wanted to ask what the hell had just happened, but she didn't, just watched as the DA walked out of the courtroom.

Jack slid his hand over her arm, and she turned back to

him. "I need to talk to you," he said. There was just something in the way he watched her.

She reached down for her briefcase and tucked his file inside. "I'm sure you do. I have a lot of questions for you, too. For one, who the hell was that judge? I've never seen him before. And, oops, they got the wrong guy? New evidence, new suspect? Like, what the fuck?" She leaned in, wondering if he'd picked up on the bite in her words. "And just like that, charges are dismissed and you're free to go? Never, ever in my career as a lawyer has that happened."

Jack just exhaled. He was still touching her and looking over her head to the back of the courtroom. "Yeah, well, it seems this was about teaching me a lesson. They're showing me that I crossed a line and need to behave, because they have six ways to Sunday to get to me and silence me."

She stared at him, feeling herself being dragged down the rabbit hole. She moved to step back, and as he ran his hand over his face, she realized there was still so much about him she didn't know.

"I'm not calling the shots in my own life," he continued. "As quickly as they can yank my life away from me, they can also give it back. Shit!" He shook his head. "It's their playbook, showing me who they control and how far their reach is. I'm so sorry, Karen, because I know you're now on their radar. We need to talk, but not here."

She didn't know what to say to him. She didn't know why, but she turned and felt a weight lift when she spotted Luke at the back of the courtroom. He was shaking his head, his expression grim. Marcus was there, too, and he motioned to her. She'd never seen him appear so rattled. She gripped her briefcase and started walking.

"Well, that was quite the shitshow," Luke said in a low

voice, looking right past her to Jack, who she knew was behind her. Marcus was holding the courtroom door open, and she kept going, walking past all of them. Marcus fell in beside her.

"Karen," Jack called out. "I need to talk to you."

Luke had turned to watch him, walking on her other side. Her brothers were there, and she knew this was as private as it was going to get.

"Well, talk," she said.

"Jack!" a man called out.

Karen turned. The man was older, gray haired, distinguished, in a brown tweed suit. He was walking toward them, his thin lips pasted into an odd smile.

"Well, this isn't good," Jack muttered as he stepped up beside her, closer, and rested his hand on her lower back.

"Who is that?" Karen said, feeling the tension in him as the man approached.

"My father," he said in a low voice, his hand still touching her. "What are you doing here?"

She hadn't expected the coldness in his voice as the older man stopped, letting his gaze linger on her. His eyes were an odd shade of brown. She couldn't see a resemblance, and she felt the awkwardness of the moment. Everything he'd said about his family left her unsettled.

"Well, you must be Karen, my son's wayward wife," the man said. "Eight years is a long time to be married and not see each other." He smiled, charming, not the image Jack had painted of him. "You managed to get yourself in quite the jam, didn't you, son?"

Karen realized it was more a statement than a question.

The man settled his gaze on Jack now, his smile gone. He leaned in and lowered his voice. "Quite the mess I had to clean up for you. I would expect a thank-you at the very least."

The unease lingered as she looked up at Jack, who was shaking his head, his lips firmed.

"A word, Jack." The man gestured, his expression one she never wanted to be on the wrong side of. He looked down at her again. "Your wife will be fine with her brothers," he said, glancing briefly to them before walking past Jack in a slow, deliberate stroll.

"Give me a minute," was all Jack said, then stepped away, off to the side.

She took in the granite pattern on the gleaming, polished floor.

"Well, isn't this what you call a plot twist?" Luke said from her other side. Both her brothers had flanked her again as they watched the father and son.

"I'm not liking this," Marcus said in a low voice.

"Uh-huh. I see the viper has slid out of the nest," Luke added.

She didn't have a clue what the man was saying to Jack, but he was now walking the other way, and Jack seemed to hesitate, looking up. He appeared rattled. Then he was striding over to her, shaking his head.

"Let's get out of here," was all he said, and he touched her arm, but she shook him off, standing firm. She turned back to see his father was now gone.

"First I want to know what the hell that was about," she said. "Did you call your father? How did he know you were here? What the fuck is this, Jack?"

He let out a heavy sigh, and his gaze lingered on each of her brothers before settling on her. "A message, a warning. I get that you want answers…" He looked up, and she found herself glancing back to see what he was looking at. A security camera?

"We all do," Luke cut in. Karen knew he was frowning, and she took in the exchange between the men.

"And I'll give them to you," Jack said to him before he directed his attention to Karen again. "Just not here."

"YOU DON'T HAVE to wait or babysit me," Karen said. "Seriously, though I appreciate you bringing some clothes for Jack. As he's out of jail now, I think we can let everything get back to normal."

Luke was leaning on her island. A hot shower was running, and she knew Jack was still in there. She took in the folded pair of Luke's jeans and T-shirt sitting on the back of the sectional, which he had picked up from their mom's. She should take them into her bedroom and leave them on her bed for Jack.

"Normal? What the fuck is normal, Karen?" he said.

"You know what I mean, before he called." She gestured behind her to the bathroom. Marcus gave a rude snort from where he stood, holding a mug, trying to figure out how to work her espresso machine. He was staring at the steel nozzle and tapping it.

"Marcus O'Connell, that's a three-thousand-dollar espresso machine you're about to break. Give me that." She walked around the island and took the mug he was holding.

"What's wrong with a twenty-dollar coffee pot?" Marcus said. She knew her brothers were both on edge. "At least I can work that, and there's no difference in the coffee."

"Before he called, Karen," Luke said, "we thought you were just our sister, not married to a man whose family walks in the shadows. They pulled off that courtroom circus, landed your hubby behind bars as a warning, and quite possibly were behind the murder of his lover. So what the fuck do you think they would do to you? That was a professional hit, planned. For all we know, this place has already been bugged and someone is watching you—because of him." Luke gestured toward the bathroom.

He and Marcus weren't helping. Her nerves were frayed.

She finished making the coffee and rested it on the island. "FYI, Marcus, there's a huge difference between a cheap coffeemaker and this."

He only shook his head and lifted his gaze to the ceiling.

"Luke, this is Montana," Karen said, "not the big city where that kind of thing happens…"

"You think you're safe anywhere?" he said.

"You know, what really bothers me is the fact that the DA, Tibo Lewis, was there, and a judge I've never seen or heard of replaced Judge Thompson with no explanation." She opened her fridge, seeing a carton of juice and a bottle of wine. She pulled out the wine and set it on the counter, then reached for a glass in the cupboard. "I need a drink. I have no beer. Can I pour you one?" she said to Luke, lifting the bottle and unscrewing the cap to pour out more than a splash. He shook his head, and she continued. "Maybe I should be asking you to explain that circus, because that's what it was. So his name is clear? Sorry for the trouble and inconvenience, Mr. Curtis, but you're free to go…"

Marcus didn't say a word, just walked around the island, glancing to the side as if listening for something.

"You really want an answer from me?" Luke said. "I don't have one to give you. There's your answer. Did Jack get a warning? Yeah, I saw it. Did it surprise me? Nope, not even a little. I've seen it before. I've learned to just follow orders, even when things happen that I can't talk about and no one would believe, either. You have no idea what really goes on behind the scenes of companies, cities, countries. I see more than I want to. I expected something to happen." Luke shrugged.

She lifted the glass of wine and just stared at her brother over the rim.

"Not the answer you were looking for, is it?" he said.

Jack had walked into the living room, a towel around his waist. He had incredible pecs, and for a second, all she could do was stare. She heard her brother clear his throat, and she stood there, feeling incredibly awkward.

"Luke's clothes." Marcus gestured as he leaned against the counter. "They're clean and should fit—sort of," he added under his breath. She didn't miss the lack of friendliness there.

Jack hesitated before reaching for the jeans and shirt, his expression priceless. "Thanks," was all he said, then flicked his gaze to Karen before walking back into her bedroom and closing her door.

"You know I'm a big girl, right? Maybe it would be best if I spoke with Jack alone. I really appreciate this, but I refuse to walk around looking over my shoulder, and you can't watch me forever."

Marcus didn't appear too interested in moving. He took a swallow of coffee. "Not until we hear what good ol'

Jack has to say and we walk him the fuck out of here. I'll even give him a ride home," he added.

The bedroom door opened, and there was Jack, unshaven still, his wet hair brushed back, wearing Luke's clothes, which were a little big on him. He let his gaze settle on her, the icy blue she remembered, but he was so different now. He was older, and so was she.

She lifted her wine. "Would you like a glass? I mean, you could probably use it."

He shook his head and took a step into the living room, and she wondered what he was thinking as he looked around at her simple furniture, the family photos on the wall, and her brothers, who had no intention of leaving. "No, it's a little early for me."

She shrugged and took a swallow.

"Well, spill it," Luke cut in, settling into his stance as he pulled his buff arms over his chest. He really was ripped.

"That was my father at the courthouse," Jack said. "Apparently, he was teaching me a lesson and letting me know the power he has. Because I'm family, I got a warning instead of a bullet. I'm sorry I dragged you into this."

"So you're saying your father is responsible for that judge showing up and the DA withdrawing charges?" Luke said.

Jack nodded and rested his hand over the back of her sectional, running his fingers over the fuzzy blue blanket tossed there. "He would've made a call. He has people who handle that for him. You start to get an idea of who's been bought, who follows orders and questions nothing. Who's the right person to make someone go away? You don't know how many levels of the system have been infiltrated. Your sister is safe now. I would really like to speak with my wife alone." He dragged his gaze from Luke to Marcus, and Karen really felt as if she were the odd woman out.

"Nah, think we'll stay right here. She's our sister, and we know fuck-all about you," Marcus said.

Jack let out a rough laugh, running his hand over the back of his head. "Fine, stay. Karen, you drink too much. It's barely noon, and that will solve nothing."

Now he was being an asshole. That had her gripping her glass and taking another swallow. She heard her brother snort a rough laugh.

"If you knew Karen, you wouldn't be saying that to her," Marcus said. "Your wife? You may be married, but that's only on paper. You know nothing about her."

"Excuse me, Marcus, but I can speak for myself," she cut in, leveling a glance his way. He only lifted his hands, evidently feeling the bite of her sharp tongue. "You know what? Jack is right. We need to talk—alone. I'm fine. Everyone's fine. I'll see you both tonight."

She put her glass down on the island and walked over to the door, feeling anger, confusion. She was too rattled to be tired. She pulled the door open and stood there as Marcus pushed away from the island and headed for Jack. For a moment, from the way Jack flinched, she wondered if he expected to be hit again. The side of his lip was still cut and bruised.

"No monkey business. That's my sister." Marcus thumped his finger against Jack's chest, and Karen lifted her gaze to the ceiling as Luke followed him to the door, where he turned and let his gaze linger long and hard on Jack.

"I don't think this is a good idea," Marcus said. "Let me toss him in the cruiser and drive him back where he came from."

Even though he pushed her buttons, Karen knew Marcus always had her back.

"No, this is my mess to fix," she said. "I'll see you tonight."

Marcus walked out, and Luke stopped in front of her and shook his head. "You call me in two hours. If you don't…"

She touched his arm, feeling the solid muscle. "Yeah, I know. You'll be back. Thanks, Luke."

Then her brothers were gone, and she closed the door, letting her hand linger a second before flicking the deadbolt just because, then turning back to a man she didn't know what she was supposed to feel for.

"Protective, aren't they?" he said.

She walked back into the kitchen, to where her glass was sitting. "We're family. We have each other's backs."

He didn't look away, and she wondered, by the face he made, if she'd hit a nerve. "You know, Karen, I made a point of knowing where you were, keeping tabs on you, making sure you were okay. I knew you were close with your family, though I'm not sure I understand that kind of loyalty and support. I also knew who you were with, which was no one."

"Right, you said you've been stalking me…"

"Watching over you," he cut in.

"Oh, that's what you call it?" She made a face as she reached for her wine, but Jack was right there, sliding it out of reach. "Hey!" she snapped.

"I also know that your go-to when you have a bad day is a glass of this. Maybe I want you completely sober to talk."

Her heart thudded, maybe from the way he watched her before he winced and looked away. "Fine, I'll leave the wine, but start talking," she said. "I don't know anything about you, Jack. The young man I fell in love with seems to be an illusion."

"I'm the same person who fell head over heels for you, Karen. That young man who found a backwoods preacher and talked you into marrying me was the real me, right here." He tapped his chest. "The man who walked out on you was playing a role so you wouldn't come looking for him. I put a target on you and thought I had protected you. I was wrong." He was shaking his head, and he glanced away, making a rude noise.

"I don't understand what your family would want with me," she said. "I'm just a simple girl from a small town. Why am I a target? Then there's Bonnie. Let's talk about her. Cards on the table, Jack. She's dead, execution style, so who did it? Your family?"

He was shaking his head again. "You're not a simple anything, Karen, but what you are is important to me. Bonnie was foolish. I cared about her, but she wouldn't leave things well enough alone, you know, poking around in a nest of snakes and thinking she wouldn't get bit. I let things slip about my family, things they've done. There was this Washington lobbyist on their payroll. My family wanted some state land because there were hot springs on it, ones they didn't want to be available to the public. It was somewhere in the mountains, a big national park. Calls were made, and all of a sudden, permits were issued and a resort was built. The property became off limits to the public. It was still government parkland, but it was suddenly controlled by my family.

"Money changed hands, a lot of money. Who was involved? A lot of people, puppets placed in the government and key industries and companies. Some high-ranking federal workers did as they were told. But it doesn't always go smoothly. A lawyer with one of the branches of government came across one of the leases and started digging, looking for a paper trail, and next thing, he was found dead. It was called a suicide even though he had two bullets in the back of his head. He was found by his six-year-old daughter."

Karen didn't know what to say. She flattened her hands on the island, and Jack rested his over them.

"I was careless with Bonnie," he said, "and that's on me. I told her too much one night, and she picked up where that lawyer had left off. I admire her for it, but she was out of her league. Who killed her? Someone in my family was likely behind it, but they never get their hands dirty. You have no idea how many lost souls do that kind of work. Soulless people can take a life and it means nothing to them. As you saw in that police file, the evidence against me was open and shut, yet just like that, my father made it all go away."

Karen pulled her hands back. "I don't understand that kind of power, Jack."

He shook his head. "I, unfortunately, do. My father knows everything about you, everything about your mom, your brothers, and your little sister."

She stepped back, a shiver running right through her. "Jack, are you telling me my family isn't safe, or I'm not safe? I'll draw up the divorce papers, you'll sign them, and then you'll tell your family I'm not a threat."

Jack was still shaking his head. "It doesn't work that way, Karen."

"Why not?" she shouted back.

"Because they just showed their hand and what they're capable of. I made a mistake eight years ago, but right now, I'm not willing to make another one and walk away from you. I can't. The only way to make sure they don't touch you or your family is for you and me to stay married, for me to make it clear you're off limits."

"You're crazy." The island was between them. He was saying the one thing she would've given anything to hear eight years earlier.

"Karen, this is the only way."

"The way for what, Jack? You'll tell your family to stay away from me, it's that simple."

"You know it's not, Karen. Maybe I'm fucking selfish, too."

Karen pushed away and walked around the island, barefoot, into the living room. Jack tracked her every move. "My brothers will kill you."

He shrugged. "Which ones?"

"Does it matter? All of them. Look, you know Luke had to practically stand guard because he gets how dangerous your family is. Apparently, he understands your world better than I do. This isn't a reason to stay married." She was shaking her head, and he was walking around the sectional toward her. He rested his hands on her shoulders and ran them down her bare arms.

"When I married you, God dammit, Karen, I was so fucking head over heels for you. Let me tell you, seeing what you've done with your life, I love you more. Maybe seeing my life about to be ripped from me, seeing the choices I've made, has shown me I don't want what they have. They want to pull my strings, put me places so I become one more of their puppets. I know enough of what they do to know I can never be that. But I'll make peace with them, Karen, so they leave you be, leave your family be."

She shut her eyes and leaned in, and he pressed a kiss to her forehead. She wanted to feel his arms around her, but she couldn't be that girl again. She pressed the flat of her hand to his chest and stepped back. "You're going to join them, aren't you? And then what, Jack?"

He shoved his hands through his damp hair, frustrated, and she moved back so he couldn't touch her again. "Your scrappy personality is what sunk me," he said. "I knew you'd never make anything easy. You have a cute place here, simple."

"You always knew how to change the subject right in the middle of an argument," she said. "I remember that, too. It used to infuriate me. Now I think it's a strategy." She pulled her arms over her chest as he settled those blue eyes on her. A smile touched his lips, and the grunt he gave sounded more like a laugh under his breath.

"Okay, fine." He nodded as if giving in. "Look, Karen, we're still married, and we're going to stay married for now. You want to be angry, hate me, go for it. I was just given a clear message, a get-out-of-jail-free card. A friend is lying in the morgue with a bullet in her head because I was living my own life, but I was playing right into their hands. I need to go home, tonight."

She let out a sigh. "Well, go." She gestured to the door.

"Karen, you don't get it. When I say I need to go home, I mean us, together. You're coming with me. I have some things I have to take care of, and I can't do it here."

"You're telling me what to do? Listen up, Jack. I'm not going anywhere…" She gestured to the door, but he was already walking toward her again with a look she hadn't seen in a long time. She thought he swore under his breath.

"Okay, bad choice of words. I have a place in Missoula. Please, pretty please, will you come with me so that I don't spend all night worrying that something has happened to you? Just one night. Will you do that one thing for me?" He held up a finger, and his voice had softened.

"Only one night?" She pulled her arms over her chest.

He fisted his hands, letting them fall to his sides. "Yes, please."

She considered it for a second, knowing she needed to call Luke before he was back there, knocking on her door. "This doesn't mean I'm going to stay married to you, Jack."

He nodded again and glanced away. "Well, let's go."

She realized he hadn't answered her. "I need to call my brother."

He let out a soft laugh and shook his head, looking down. "Of course you do. By all means, call him." Jack pulled his arms over his chest and then flicked his gaze to her. "And, Karen?"

She hesitated, seeing how serious he'd suddenly become. "Yes, Jack?"

"In case I didn't say it, thank you."

Thirteen

"YOU'RE PRETTY QUIET OVER THERE," Jack said from behind the wheel of her simple no frills Honda. "Everything good with your family?"

In the passenger seat, Karen took in the darkened highway, unable to shake her uncertainty and excitement, which she knew wasn't good for her. "If you want to know what Luke said, just ask." She pulled at her cream sweater, which she wore overtop a simple blue sleeveless cotton dress, and kicked off her black pumps. Her toes were bare.

Jack made a face and glanced at her. She had no idea what he was thinking. "Do I need to worry about him coming after you?"

She wondered if he had any idea what he was saying. "It would be Marcus and Owen, and maybe Ryan, coming after me. Luke would be one step ahead, waiting for you."

He stilled, and even in the darkened vehicle, she could see the hesitation. "Should I be expecting trouble?" he said, gripping the steering wheel.

She lifted her chin, looking straight out the windshield toward passing headlights on the other side of the road.

Luke would have shared even less with her family than she had. She said nothing.

"Karen, are you fucking with me?"

She let out a sigh and shrugged as she turned back to Jack. "No. Don't worry. I saved you this time. Told Luke you didn't want to wait to get your car out of impound in the morning, so we were driving up to Missoula tonight. Of course, he didn't think it was a good idea, me going off alone with you. And he reminded me what happened the last time I did."

He glanced her way again and shook his head, but he said nothing.

"Marcus has your address," she said. "He knows where you live, all the cars you own, everything he could find out about you on paper. So if they don't hear from me by seven tomorrow morning, well, they know where to come." She gestured ahead. "But then, I only packed an overnight bag with a change of clothes. I plan on being back on the road in the morning. I have commitments, Jack, a law practice, clients…"

The truth was that Luke had said only one thing to her: *You better know what the fuck you're doing, Karen!*

Lights in the distance meant they were getting closer to Missoula.

"Karen, you'll have to reschedule what you can for later in the week," Jack said. "You can't go back tomorrow. I can have movers pack up your things and bring them to my house…" He seemed lost in thought. "I just have a feeling there's something in the wind, and I don't want to leave anything to chance. I'll send someone to get my car out of the impound."

She just stared at him, wondering what the hell he was talking about. "I have a bag in the back, an overnight one, with a pair of sweats for tomorrow. I have one change of clothes. Let me remind you what you said: one night so you can take care of a few things."

He let out a sigh that sounded too much like frustration and shook his head. As he flicked on her signal light, she took in the sign for a community outside Missoula. "Okay, I shouldn't have said one night," he said. "I've been running everything I have to take care of through my head. We'll talk more when we get home, but I've got to make some calls, fix some things. I'll have a better idea in a couple days. It will be easier from here. It'll be fine. You'll see." He had to be messing with her, but she could see how serious he was as he took the offramp.

"Get this through your head," she said. "I'm not leaving Livingston. I'm going back tomorrow morning. What is going through your mind? That we're married so now, eight years later, you're going to suddenly manage my life? It's evident you don't know me, because if you did, you wouldn't expect me to drop everything because you want to stay married, as if my life and what I do isn't as important as you. You're not having a conversation with me, either. It's like you've decided this and I'm supposed to fall in line. Have you always been like this? Evidently, I don't know you, either—but then, how could I? In case I haven't made myself absolutely clear, this trip is to pick up your things, one night only. If you think I'm going to say goodbye to my life, close up my business, and move to Missoula, away from my family, you're mistaken."

She reached for her cell phone in the pocket of her purse, which was at her feet on the floor, as Jack pulled off the road and into a gated community with big houses and big yards.

"Who are you calling?" He let out a heavy sigh.

"None of your business," she snapped.

He turned his head sharply, then looked back at the

residential street. "Karen, I know you have a life in Livingston and your family is there. I get it, I really do— but there's more at stake, and right now I need you to be a little reasonable and flexible. How could I have forgotten how stubborn you are?"

She just stared at him as he pulled into a long circular driveway. The house was two stories, with what she thought was a three-car garage, and from the outside it looked to be more than three thousand square feet. Huge, way too big for a single man.

He turned off her car and yanked the door open, then turned to her for a second, on edge. She didn't remember him being the kind of guy who would expect her to just drop everything for him.

"This isn't about me being stubborn, Jack. I will never be told what to do, and I'm not going to walk away from everything I've worked for, not for anyone. Were you always this way?"

He shook his head. "What way?" Under the overhead light, he took her in, then made a rude noise and stepped out, giving the door a shove closed behind him before she could answer him. She shoved her feet back into her heels, and she too stepped out as he walked around the back and opened the trunk to pull out her overnight bag.

"You're a chauvinist," she said.

The outside lights of the house flicked on—she supposed he had security lighting—as he started toward it. He stopped, letting out another sigh of frustration, and turned back to her.

"Sorry," he said. "I'm tired, and I'm not used to clearing what I'm thinking and needing to do with anyone." He looked out to the yard and nodded to the house. "Can we do this inside?"

He started walking to the front door again, a double set

of dark wood doors with glass at either side. He punched in numbers on the keypad and then opened the door, glancing back to her.

She looked back once to her car before following him in. The inside light flicked on, and she took in the impressive front entrance, the vaulted ceiling, the stairs, which reminded her of something from the Old South. This was definitely a key feature of the house. She closed the door behind her, her heels clicking on the stone tile as she turned.

He dropped her bag off to the side and tossed her car keys on the hall table, then looked right at her.

"You live here alone?" she said.

He only nodded, then took one step toward her, then another, until he was standing in front of her, resting his hands on her shoulders and dragging them down, a gentle touch. He reached behind her and locked the door. He needed to shave, and his icy blue eyes seemed to flicker and soften as he traced his fingers over her chin. She was positive he was going to kiss her. She took a step to the side, her heart hammering, and his hand fell away.

"Yes, Karen, I live here alone. So you think I'm a chauvinist, really?" He wasn't smiling. She made herself look at him.

"You think I'm going to fall in line?"

He just shook his head and said, "I need to change." Then he started up the stairs, leaving her standing where she was, hearing the echoes of a big house, a clock ticking, she thought, in the background.

So what did she do but follow him up? She ran her hand over the dark railing, taking in the green and brown carpet runner. The house was likely bigger than she'd first thought, she realized as she topped the landing, seeing art on the walls down the hallway, lined with four doors.

She kept walking to the room at the end where Jack had gone. The double doors were open, and she stopped just inside the doorway, taking in the spaciousness, with a king-size four poster, a dresser, end tables, and two ottomans in front of a gas fireplace. There was Jack in a huge walk-in closet, and she wasn't sure what to say as he flicked on the light to reveal that it alone was the size of her bedroom.

She didn't have to follow him in to know he had a lot of clothes, really nice things. Everything about the furnishings of the house told her that money clearly wasn't a problem for him. The window overlooked the back, and solar lights revealed a large yard with a covered outdoor pool.

She heard a rustle behind her and turned to see him in a pair of dark pants, pulling on a navy long-sleeved dress shirt. His eyes connected with hers for a second, and she could see the edge to him. He appeared angry, upset. Good. So was she.

Then he just shook his head without saying a word and started out of the bedroom, leaving her there. She wished he'd say something, considering this silence gave her nothing to fight with. She stepped out of the bedroom and looked over the rail to see he was already down the stairs.

"You're going to just walk away? Jack, seriously, have you always been this dismissive?" she called out, but he had disappeared down the hall.

She wasn't about to be the girl who let a guy blow her off like this, so she hurried as fast as she could down the stairs in her heels, following him to a large open kitchen, a chef's dream. It seemed to have everything: a huge island with a gas stove, the same vaulted ceilings. It was open to a family room, which had an impressive stone fireplace that drew her attention. But then, so did everything in this house. The furnishings were tasteful pastels with two leather recliners. She wondered who had designed the place for him.

At the same time, it wasn't lost on her that he wasn't answering or fighting back.

He pulled out steaks from the fridge and set them on the counter, then opened a door to reveal a walk-in pantry. Karen crossed her arms, feeling so unsettled. The silent treatment was something she'd given others when she was hurt and angry. Jack walked back out with potatoes in hand and set them on the counter.

"You're making dinner?" She gestured toward the steaks.

"We need to eat," he said, an edge in his voice. "I'm hungry. I'm sure you are, too."

He scrubbed two potatoes in the sink at the island, saying nothing, then turned on the oven, poked the potatoes with a fork, and tossed them in to bake before looking to the side out the window. He flicked his gaze right to her as he rested his hands on the island.

"You're beautiful, Karen," he said, "and I've loved you from afar for years, but don't ever talk to me like that again. I'm not dismissing you. I'm very aware of what you've created, what you've done. I'm proud of you, but hear me when I say it's impossible for me to move to Livingston. It can't happen. I have a house here, a law practice I'm taking over with five junior partners and a staff of ten. I was leaving the DA's office anyway, just got pushed out sooner than planned. I can easily move you into a position here. It's about practicality, among other things. Don't make this difficult."

The way he said it, all humor gone, it was as if he wasn't going to hear her, and she realized he didn't get it.

"There you go again, saying you can't, and this is the

way it has to be, end of story," she said. "Anything else?" She hadn't meant to be so sarcastic, but she didn't like anyone telling her what to do. "You tell me not to talk to you that way… You're kidding, right? Because you *are* being dismissive, and I'm getting the very distinct feeling you believe I'm your subordinate, that my one-woman show as a small-town lawyer is something to turn your nose up at. Are we taking a step back decades, saying because you're a man, everything must center around you, and because I'm a woman, I need to make sure I don't steal the spotlight? What I do is very important, and you evidently have no idea who I am."

From the way he was looking at her, she wondered if he was about to dismiss her again.

"What you have here is nice," she said, "but it's not something I'm striving for, because the kind of people I help would never be able to pay me what I'd need to make to buy something like this, let alone furnish it. I like to think I'm the kind of lawyer who's making a difference for the average person who needs someone like me, the kind of clients who couldn't afford to sit in the lobby at your firm even if I were, as you might want, a junior clerk there. Your hourly rates probably start at, what, two or three hundred dollars?" She gestured to him, then crossed her arms, feeling uneasy but ready to fight.

"Five hundred," he said from where he leaned on the island, "but there's room for negotiation on a case-by-case basis. Again, Karen, this has nothing to do with me being more important. I have more than you, yes. But I won't apologize for having all this, and I need you to be reasonable. I'm not asking you to give up helping people."

"The people I help can't afford five hundred dollars an hour."

He was shaking his head again.

"You know what?" she said before he could interject. "Maybe this isn't a great idea. You're not hearing me. I love my job, where I live, and the way I practice law. Your life is here, and I'm starting to get the feeling you expect me to fit into it. How about I leave now? I have my car, and now you're home."

He walked around the island, shaking his head. "No, Karen, you can't leave. Don't put words in my mouth, either. I'm not saying what you do is less important, and I've certainly never said you're beneath me. Don't be ridiculous. I know what you've done, and I'm impressed—hell, blown away by some of the cases you've handled, the clients you've fought for, clients no one else would waste their time on. Maybe I admire you for fighting for the underdog. But I never took you for the kind of woman who would cut and run when it got tough. You're a fighter. That much I know about you. Look, let's just have some dinner, and we'll talk. I'm tired and hungry. When I'm tired and hungry, I'm not reasonable. Please..."

Jack walked around the island, pulling his hand over his chin with a scrape of whiskers. He stopped in front of her and slid his hands over her shoulders, then over her cheeks and into her hair. "How about a glass of wine?" he said.

Damn, she'd forgotten how smooth he could be. She had to remind herself that he was the kind of man who could talk her into anything if she wasn't careful.

"Thought you said I drink too much."

He winced and shook his head. "I'm talking about just a glass, one, not the bottle."

She should say no, walk out the door, and get in her car and drive back to Livingston. "I'm not the same stupid girl you married—and even when you married me, I was never the kind of girl who would fall in line and follow you anywhere or put all my dreams on hold. If that's what you're looking for, that's not me. I have a life, one I'm not suddenly uprooting because you say I have to."

He scrubbed his hands over his face again. Evidently, she was pushing all of his buttons.

The doorbell chimed, echoing through the house. Jack glanced toward the front.

"You expecting someone?" Karen said.

"Nope," was all he said as he started to the door, an edge still in his voice.

She followed him, heels clicking, pulling at her sweater, feeling the unease again, the knot that always tightened when she went out of her comfort zone. She watched as he looked through the peephole, then unlocked the door and pulled it open. A man was there, dark hair, medium build and height, in a dark sports jacket and pants.

"Well, there you are." The man gestured to the driveway with his thumb. "Whose piece-of-shit car is that? Please tell me it's a delivery person dropping off dinner or something…" He stepped inside, handsome, around the same age as Jack.

"Pierce, seriously?" Jack said as he closed the door.

The man was now staring right at her. "Hello," he said with some amusement, a smile tugging at the corners of his mouth. "And who might you be?"

Her arms were crossed again, and she fisted her hands. "I'm Karen O'Connell, and that piece of shit is my car. And no, I'm not a delivery driver—other than delivering Jack home," she added as she stepped forward, though she didn't hold out her hand.

Jack was shaking his head again. "Pierce, this is Karen, my wife." He gestured toward her, flicking his icy blue eyes at her. "And, Karen, this is my cousin, Pierce Curtis."

Fourteen

SHE FOUND herself seated to the right of Jack at the head of his dining room table. The room was just as impressive as the rest of the house, with its own fireplace and glass doors that led out to the patio by the pool. She was having a hard time understanding how Jack lived this way as a single man. She had counted four bedrooms, five bathrooms. The house had everything, and it just seemed too much—in her mind, anyway. When she married him, they'd been young, living in a small, plain apartment, much like the average couple just starting out, with nothing to their name. What she was seeing now made her feel out of place. This was a side of Jack she didn't know.

"Wow, I still can't get over the fact that you're married, and to such a beautiful woman," Pierce said. He talked a lot, but under all that charm, she wondered if perhaps he knew Jack in a way she never would.

She lifted her glass of water, wishing for wine. Jack had brushed off her questions after his cousin arrived, and unfortunately she only had more now. She realized they were both staring at her as she chewed her steak, rare. Why hadn't she protested when he didn't ask her how she wanted her steak cooked?

"Sorry, did I miss something?" She gestured to them with her fork, unsure what to make of the odd exchange. Jack appeared uncomfortable.

"I asked what you did for a living," Pierce said, leaning in.

"I'm a lawyer," she said, gesturing toward herself while still holding her knife and fork. Jack's hand came to rest over hers, and he appeared annoyed now. Right, table manners. Apparently, that bothered him. She put her knife and fork down on either side of the undercooked steak.

"Wow, a lawyer. I'm impressed. What, corporate, tax…?" Pierce looked over to Jack, who was focused on cutting a piece of steak and shoving it in his mouth. He swallowed, not looking at her.

"Karen does a little of everything," he replied. "Whatever's needed. Lots of small-time criminal cases for the down and out who find themselves in trouble, as well." It was a slap-down she hadn't expected from him.

She was stuck on "small-time." "Yes, I do a little of everything," she said, "but mainly criminal law for those who don't have anyone else to help them—and can't afford five hundred an hour, or whose fathers can't call in favors and buy their way out of a jam. I assure you, to them, it's not small-time. They're fighting for their very survival."

Jack coughed. She picked up her knife and fork, knowing he was looking right at her.

"Ah, I see, a bleeding heart," Pierce said. "How wonderful."

Karen flicked her gaze across the table, wondering whether Jack's cousin's amusement was at her expense. She shoved her fork into her baked potato and took a bite.

"So you work for basically nothing?" Pierce said. He didn't have the same icy blue eyes as Jack; they were a light shade of brown, and she was having a hard time seeing a resemblance. "I guess someone has to do it for the lower class. Wow, that will look good for you. Brilliant on your part, Jack." He leaned back in the dining chair and glanced at Jack as if what Karen had said was entertaining.

She found herself looking toward the hall, where the door was. What the hell was she doing there?

"Pierce, knock it off," was all Jack said. He didn't look her way. She couldn't help feeling as if she were a shiny new toy that had lost its charm.

"Did Jack tell you how we met?" she said. Pierce frowned, and Jack stilled. "I mean after the eight-year absence, after he basically told me to fuck off. Well, he called me again."

"Karen," Jack said rather sharply.

"Don't you think your cousin would like to know about the jam you found yourself in, the one you called me to get you out of?" She leaned in, feeling her adrenaline pulse as she squeezed her knife and fork. Her gaze landed on Pierce, who appeared as if he had a front-row seat to a comedy. "You want to call me a bleeding heart? I'd say making a difference for those who are truly victims just makes me a decent human being."

Jack dumped his knife and fork on his plate with a clatter. "Karen, enough," he said. The way he looked at her, she sensed he was ready to shut her down.

"It's not enough, Jack. I'm not just playing around with the law. I'm actually making a difference, being the kind of lawyer you're supposed to be, trying to right the wrongs of this ridiculous broken system…"

"Helping lost causes?" Pierce cut in, then cleared his throat. "That doesn't really mean you're credible."

She leaned back and set her knife and fork down, then reached for her napkin on her lap and wiped her face before dumping it on her plate. She was done with this beat-down.

"You're an asshole," she said to Jack, "and I'm done with whatever this is." She gestured to him and his cousin.

When she moved to slide her chair back, Pierce said, "Well, on that note, as entertaining as this is, I think I'm going to leave and let you two work this out." He stood, his suit jacket still unbuttoned. "Thanks for an entertaining dinner. Karen, a pleasure. Jack, I want to know more about this eight-year lapse in your marriage. Sounds like quite the story. Oh, and before I forget, you'll be at your dad's tomorrow. I understand the partners are coming in."

Jack leaned back and inclined his head. She didn't know what to make of how he'd pulled into himself. A chill lingered. "I'll be there," was all he said. Karen stared in horror, hearing Pierce's footsteps until the door closed. Still Jack said nothing.

"You want to explain to me what that was about?" Karen said, taking in a man who was more a stranger than someone she'd loved and hated for so long. "You know, when I married you as a girl, I knew I was nothing in your shadow, and after you walked out, the way you treated me, it took a while for me to be able to hold my head high. I've had to tell myself not to feel humiliated, especially with that restraining order—which, by the way, is still in force. You know, I'm a good person, decent, loving. I make a difference. I am somebody.

"But congratulations. This evening with your cousin was quite the show. You're purely arrogant, trying to manage me, put me in my place. I don't know this game, Jack, and I don't want to know it or be part of it. You're going to see your father tomorrow, and I take it these part-ners are the same men you talked about so passionately, the ones responsible for killing Bonnie and leaving you rotting in jail. These men do the kinds of things I'm not okay with. So thanks for dinner, though the steak was a little undercooked for me. Where I come from, we ask how someone wants her steak done."

She didn't know what to make of the way he was watching her, unsettlingly, as she slid back her chair and stood up. The long dining table, silverware, and artwork were both disconcerting and unwelcoming. The tension was thick.

She gestured toward the front door. "I'm going home. Goodnight, Jack." She took a step.

"Karen, you can't leave," Jack said, his chair scraping as he stood.

She kept walking, giving her head a shake. "Of course I can, and I am. It's this thing called free will, and I very much still have mine. I'll never hand it over. Not sure what this is, but I'm not having any part of it."

He was walking around the table and gesturing to her. "Just wait a second." There was an edge to his voice. "You don't get it, Karen. That was entirely for show. Pierce didn't show up here just because. I didn't know who would come tonight, but I had a feeling someone would. He was here to make sure I'm falling in line, that I'm doing what my father demanded. Yeah, I'm free because of him, and I was in trouble because of him. Life isn't black and white. The fact is, Karen, they need to be sure you aren't another Bonnie, trying to dig up something or cause trouble that would embarrass the family. You saw the photos!

"They will not take my word that you're not a problem. They will fucking dissect your life and your family's. I guarantee you someone has already searched your office and home for anything that could lead them to believe you'll be a problem for them. It scares the shit out of me that something could happen to you!" He jammed his hands in his hair, tightly wound. "Dammit! I need you to just trust me. Maybe I came off as arrogant and high-handed. I'm sorry, but I'm not sorry if it means keeping you alive. Just give me some room to figure out how to handle this without coming at me the way you are. I'm not stepping back into the family. I'm doing damage control that will keep you safe. I need to figure out a way to do this right, because I screwed up eight years ago."

He was now right in front of her, and for a moment, she thought he'd touch her, but he just shook his head, letting out a heavy sigh as if at a loss. "I fell head over heels in love with you, and I never stopped loving you," he said, then took a step back, and she didn't have a clue what to say. Passion radiated from him, and for a moment she thought she could believe him.

"The restraining order is no longer in force," he said. "I had it dismissed before we left Livingston, when you were packing that overnight bag. I put a call in to my firm."

"I don't know what you want from me," she said. "This is a game I don't know the rules to, and I have no intention of playing it."

He really was unsettled. "You can't walk out the door, Karen."

She shook her head. "I can," she said, and she went to take a step around him, but his hand went right to her arm. He was so damn close.

"Please, Karen, I'm stumbling around like an ass, trying to figure out how to navigate this minefield. I never expected to be on the wrong side of my family. I know I'm screwing up, but I don't mean to, not with you. Please don't walk out that door. You have no idea how dangerous they are. I need you to trust me." He was still touching her.

"That's asking too much, Jack."

"I love you, Karen. I always have."

She went to look away, to shut her eyes, because he was slipping under her skin, and it had nearly killed her before. "It can't work, Jack," she said, but he was brushing the back of his fingers over her face, and she leaned into him.

"I want it to," he said. He settled his hands over her cheeks, was right in front of her, and rested his forehead against hers before pressing a kiss to her lips. It was unexpected. He let it linger as she reached up and touched his wrists, holding on.

"I won't be handled or treated like nothing, game or not," she said once he had pulled away. "I'll give you the night to figure it out, Jack, but you need to do it in a way that gets you away from them, not closer. I have a voice. What I do isn't of less importance. I will not live here. Livingston is my home, my family is there, I work there. So you need to figure out a way to make your family understand that. With what just happened, there's no way I'm going to sit idly by and pretend. I'm not a woman who will stand in the shadows. Find another way to fix this."

He sighed and slid his arms around her, and she set her hands against the solid wall of his chest and shut her eyes for a second, because she'd never believed she would feel Jack holding her again. "You may come to like living here if you give it time, give it a chance," he said.

She went to push back, and this time he didn't fight her.

Looking down at her, his gaze had softened, but he hadn't stepped back. He nodded, and an odd smile touched his lips. "I'm tired," he said. "How about we table this part of the discussion until after a good night's sleep?"

"I won't change my mind, Jack."

He glanced away and then back to her with a heavy sigh. "Yeah, I'm beginning to remember that about you."

CHAPTER
Fifteen

THE WAY he kissed her shoulder had her stirring from a deep sleep. For a second, as she blinked in the early morning light, feeling his hand running up her back, she had forgotten where she was. The touch of him was even better than she remembered. How could she have forgotten Jack was an incredible lover? With each kiss, each touch, his passion had reached her just as it had eight years earlier. She shut her eyes and sat up, pulling her knees toward her, covering her breasts with the sheet. Jack was leaning there, running his hand up her back gently and tenderly as if he remembered how sensitive she was to his touch.

"What's wrong?" he said.

She turned to the bedside table, where the digital clock read 5:38 a.m. "We can't just pick up where we left off, Jack. Too much time has passed, and I'm not the same starry-eyed girl who will follow you anywhere."

The bedding rustled, and she glanced over her shoulder to Jack, who was now sitting up at the edge of the bed, his back to her. He let out a heavy sigh of frustration.

"Karen, it seems you don't want to try, no matter what I say or do." He stood up and flicked on the bedside light. "My father is sending his plane to pick us up this morning," he said, and stood, naked, and turned away. He walked into the bathroom without looking back. He was absolutely breathtaking, his naked ass, his body, but at the same time, she wanted to pull her hair out at his arrogance. This was a side of him she hadn't remembered.

It took her a second to realize what he was saying. The shower was running, and she felt as if he were once again about to yank the rug from under her. She tossed back the covers and spotted her clothes tossed in a heap over one of the two chairs in front of the fireplace. She picked up his dress shirt from the stool and slipped it on, just something she needed to do. The vulnerability he stirred inside her had come out of nowhere.

She stared for a moment at the open door to the ensuite, where soft light drifted out, and she pulled his shirt closed over her breasts as she strode into the spacious room. Jack stood in the large walk-in shower, his hand pressed against the tile, his head leaning forward under the spray.

"It's amazing how you talked me into sleeping with you, staying the night," she said. "For a moment, you had me believing you wouldn't do this, telling me to fall in line."

He was staring at her through the glass door, water running down him. "What the hell are you talking about?" he said. She wondered if he always sounded so terse in the morning.

She leaned against the sink. "Your father's plane is picking us up? You did say that, right, a private plane? I'm wondering when you asked me to go with you. It seems hard for you to inform me of your plans. It's as if you expect me to fall in line and say, 'Yes, sir.'"

His gaze lingered a second, and then he blinked as he smoothed his hair back and made a face. "You're misreading the situation," he said. "He sent me a text before I woke you, a summons. He expects to see me with you. Unfortunately, neither of us has a choice." He opened the door to the shower, and she realized he expected her to just walk in there to him, but she pulled his shirt tighter around her and stayed where she was.

"You seem to forget I always have a choice—to stay, to go…"

"Karen, fuck, I'm sorry." He turned and walked back under the spray, the door still open, before looking back to her and wiping the water from his face. He let out a heavy sigh. "You're right. I'm sorry, Karen. Please help me out here." He softened his voice and pressed his hand to the open door. "I misspoke. My father texted, or rather, his assistant did, telling me his plane is on its way and we're expected to be at the airfield by seven. The family will be there, all of them, to meet you. I'm freaking out a bit because they know, or will know, what you mean to me. Karen, they won't hesitate to use you and how important you are to me to their advantage. I suspect they want something. Remember the case I wouldn't drop at the DA's office against the senator for insider trading?"

She nodded, seeing the worry he'd been trying to hide. "Vaguely."

"It was why I was pushed out. It came down from above. It's how it works when they can't get you to fold: They get rid of you. He'll be there today. Please, Karen, come with me." He was holding his hand out to her from the shower.

She let his shirt fall to the floor. His gaze lingered on

her as she walked to him and hesitated only a second before slipping her hand in his. He pulled her under the hot spray, and she heard the click of the shower door and felt his arms around her.

"Now was that so hard?" she said, and patted his chest.

He glanced up and let out a rough laugh. "Oh, dear God, Karen, you're going to be the end of me." Then he leaned down and kissed her, moving her against the tile wall. "I just need to ask one thing of you today."

She let her hands linger over his chest, feeling the hardness, his heart thudding. "Am I going to have a problem with it?"

He didn't laugh. His gaze had turned serious. "We're walking into a vipers' nest. The average person sees my family as accomplished professionals and businessmen, with wives who head up charities and children that go to private schools. But these people will never be our friends or confidants, and spending time with them is like navigating a minefield. It's why I stayed away and tried to get you to hate me. I'm going to apologize now for everything I do or say there, for being an ass or sounding arrogant or condescending, as I won't have time to pull you aside and ask you or explain it to you. Please just trust me today."

"That's asking a lot, Jack. Being uncertain and walking into something without a plan doesn't work well for me."

He nodded, his hand pressed to the wall of the shower behind her. "I'm well aware, but I promise you, Karen, my only objective today is to get my family out of both of our lives and to make it clear that I will not be a puppet for them, and neither will you. How I manage that, though…" He shook his head, and she slid her hand over the whiskers he still needed to shave.

"So what's the plan?" she said.

"I haven't worked that out yet. Any ideas, let me know.

There's only one thing, Karen, that I need you to be aware of."

"And that is?"

"That I guarantee the minute we walk out of here, the minute we step on my dad's plane, someone will be listening to everything you and I say to each other."

Now she really was unsettled. "You're serious?"

"Deadly," he said. "Welcome to my family."

THOUGH THE SUN HAD RISEN, Karen was still on edge, sitting in the back of a black town car beside Jack, her fingers linked with his. Her legs were crossed, her bare feet tucked into her black pumps, and she was wearing the same blue dress she had the day before, her stomach in knots.

Jack gestured to the gated property at the end of the half-mile private driveway and said, "I grew up here." He leaned in, she thought to press a kiss to her cheek, but instead whispered, "Just follow my lead."

He reached for her hand again as the driver stopped in front of the electronic gates, which slid open, and then sped through. Trees lined the long driveway. She'd never realized this part of Spokane existed. The house had appeared around a bend in the distance, more a mansion than a house, bigger than anything she'd ever seen. A fountain out front was surrounded by parked cars, the kind she'd never be able to afford.

Her tension built, and maybe Jack knew, as he

squeezed her hand. Damn, he was so good looking in that navy suit and light blue tie, clean shaven. He smiled, leaning in again. "Relax. You're beautiful, brilliant, and I love you." This time, he pressed a kiss to her forehead as the car stopped.

Someone opened Jack's door, and Karen listened to the splash of water, taking in the size of the fountain. A young dark-haired man in a red vest and white shirt held her door open, as well. Jack was already walking around the car to her, and he held out his hand. Why was she so damn nervous?

"You grew up here. I guess that explains a lot," she said. "This isn't a home, Jack. This is an institution."

"There you go again, you and your smart mouth. Guess you know why I came looking for you," he said as they stopped outside the impressive front door, carved with ornate figures of lions in battle.

"Remind me again what we're doing and what I promised you?" she said.

Jack hadn't knocked or even reached for the door, but she heard footsteps, as if someone knew they were there. "Be nice, smile, and if you want to give someone a piece of your mind, please don't. I know you can hold your own, but today I'm asking you not to."

The door opened before she could respond, revealing an older man with thinning hair in a dark suit. "Mr. Jack, it's been a long time. Welcome home."

"Thank you, Reggie. This is my wife, Karen."

She hadn't expected the slight bow, as if she were someone of importance.

"Welcome, Mrs. Curtis."

She wanted to correct him, but Jack squeezed her hand as they stepped inside a dark wood entryway with a marble floor. Straight ahead was the most impressive wide staircase she'd ever seen.

"Mrs. Curtis, seriously, Jack?" she said as she leaned in.

He laughed under his breath and pressed a kiss to her forehead when she looked up. "Thanks for not blowing a gasket."

She tapped his arm, leaning close, hearing voices, taking in this mausoleum. Her heels echoed down a long hallway into a grand ballroom, with tables of food and servants carrying trays and four sets of double glass doors, wide open, leading out back. She had no idea how many people were there, women, children, and men. The back held a stone patio, an Olympic swimming pool, and grass and trees, with not another house in sight.

"Holy shit, Jack. I don't understand this. You grew up here?"

He only shook his head, as a tall, slender man with white hair, wearing a light gray suit, was striding over.

"Jack, great to see you," he said and held out his hand.

Jack shook it, still holding hers, keeping her right there beside him. "Senator, heard you were going to be here," he said.

She let her gaze linger on the man, distinguished, wondering if this was the Senator in question criminal laws didn't apply to.

"This is my wife, Karen," Jack said.

The man didn't offer to shake her hand. "Oh, she's beautiful." He actually winked, and it felt slimy. "Heard you were hiding her away from all of us. Lucky man, Jack." He touched Jack's arm. "Could I borrow your husband for a moment, little lady? I promise I'll send him right back."

Karen gritted her teeth and pulled her hand from

Jack's. "It's fine. I'll get something to drink." She ran her hand over Jack's arm, and his gaze lingered, and she recognized something she'd seen a few times, that mask he slipped on.

"I'll be right back," was all he said before stepping off to the side with the senator.

A few people were looking Karen's way as she started back to the open doors. The food was just inside, and a waiter with a tray of drinks was coming out.

"Wine, ma'am?" he asked as he stopped.

She knew it would help, but it would give her courage she didn't need. "Actually, just a glass of water."

"Of course, I'll get that for you." He started back inside over to a bar.

Karen couldn't shake the awkwardness. When a hand touched her back, she jumped and turned.

"I'm so sorry," said Jack's father. "I didn't mean to scare you, Karen."

She'd never forget him, his short gray hair, the shape of his face, which did, in a way, resemble a much older Jack, and cold brown eyes that offered her no welcome or warmth. He was in a light blue dress shirt, no tie, with a light brown sports jacket overtop.

"That's all right, Mr. Curtis." She offered a tight smile.

"Randall, please. After all, we are family." He was smiling down at her, then extended his hand in front of him. "Was hoping to have a word with you." He gestured inside.

Karen glanced back to Jack, who didn't seem happy with whatever the senator was saying to him.

"Don't worry about Jack," Randall said. "He'll find you." Then he held out his arm, a gentlemanly move, one she hadn't expected. She glanced back again, willing Jack to look her way, but he didn't, so she slipped her hand on his father's arm, and he walked inside with her.

"So you and Jack are becoming re-acquainted with each other," he said. "Oh, don't worry about answering that. Body language doesn't lie. Anyone with eyes can see he'd kill for you. You have always been the one he loved."

Her heart was thudding as he walked her over to the bar.

"Would you like a glass of the pinot grigio? It's from one of our islands," he said. "I know your fondness for whites, usually Chablis, but I assure you this one from our vineyard is exceptional."

The bartender filled a glass, and Karen let her hand fall away as he held it out to her.

"I just want a glass of water," she said.

Randall had thick brows, and his eyes sparkled with something mischievous. "Nonsense," he said. "This is a celebration. I insist."

Where the hell was Jack? She took the wine, and Randall's smile widened, wolflike. He was waiting for her to taste it, so she did.

"Yes, very nice," she said, then set the glass on the bar. "Could I have a glass of water, please?"

The bartender looked over to Randall, who gave a nod as if his permission were needed. A glass appeared with ice and a lemon, and Karen lifted it and took a swallow.

"Thank you," she said to the young bartender, who only nodded.

"Shall we?" Jack's father gestured to the hallway, and she fell in beside him in a slow walk, wondering what he wanted from her.

"I wondered how long Jack would fight his feelings for you," he said. "He always was a sensitive boy, too sensitive for his own good, and I could never tell him what to do. I had plans for him, all laid out, but he would thwart them at every turn. That's what you have to look forward to. Kids, you know, challenging their parents. Sort of the same trouble you had with your mother."

A shiver ran up her spine and Karen squeezed her glass.

He chuckled softly and touched her back again. "Mothers and daughters," he said. He knew more than she was comfortable with about something she'd never shared with anyone, even Jack.

"Well, as you said, kids, right?" She lifted her gaze down the dark wood hallway, with closed doors and rich artwork. A knight's armor was displayed in a corner at the end.

"Oh, you'll make sure my son is never bored. So you're not interested in Jack's life? You want to stay in your small town instead, working cases no one else wants. You know Jack will follow you, and that's fine for a while."

Her heart was hammering, and she was scrambling to figure out what to say. "I don't understand," she said. "For a while—and then what?"

He tsked under his breath. "Let's see. You'll both have fun, and then I expect you'll start having children. Sometimes grandchildren are the ones who carry our hopes when their parents disappoint us. Jack likes to think he's smarter than all of us, but he's wrong. You know Jack isn't the first Curtis to marry outside the family?"

Karen lifted her chin as they stopped at the end of the hall, the mouth of another dimly lit hallway. She had no idea where it led, but it was taking her further from the man she loved. Maybe that was why her heart was hammering.

"Sometimes lessons are learned the hard way," Randall

said. "I had a sister who thought she'd break away, share some things that are not to be shared with no one. She ran off with a boy from New Jersey. My father warned her nothing good would come of it. They were both found stabbed to death in their small house. Apparently, she was pregnant, and whoever broke in cut the baby out. They never did find the remains of the child. The horrors that happen in places like that! A gruesome scene. If only she'd listened to my father…"

"Karen, there you are," Jack called out.

She turned to him, and the glass of water slipped from her hand and shattered at her feet. "Oh, I'm so sorry," she said, staring down, realizing she was shaking.

"Don't worry your pretty little head," Randall said. "I'll have someone clean this up."

Jack reached for her arm and helped her past the glass and the water. His father was already walking back down the hall. "You're trembling," he said. "What happened?" She thought he swore under his breath, and his hand slid tighter around her. "What were you doing with my father?"

She only shook her head, and he turned her and pulled her against him. "He found me outside and just started talking," she said. "Can we go, please?" She was a strong woman, but Jack had been right; she wasn't prepared in any way for his family.

He glanced down the hall where his father had gone, then back to her. "Yeah, sure we can. What did he say to you, Karen?" He made her look up at him, and she could see the worry there, but at the same time, she couldn't make herself repeat it.

"I think it was a message for you more than me," she said. "Let's just go, please."

He let his gaze linger a second, then nodded. "Yeah,

I'm done here anyway." He pulled her closer to him, holding her tight. "I love you."

She nodded, because she realized now how close Jack was to ending up just like his father's sister. She lifted her chin and said, "I love you, too."

CHAPTER
Seventeen

"ONE ICE-COLD CHABLIS. I even added a couple ice cubes for you," said Suzanne as she handed Karen a glass where she sat on Ryan and Jenny's front porch. Night had settled, and her lingering tension had finally left. "The bottle's inside, but Ryan said if you want more, he's going to have to send Luke out to the store."

"Thank you," Karen said. She welcomed the evening and her family. "You have no idea how much I was looking forward to this." She took a sip and nearly groaned, kicking off her pumps, which felt as if they'd been glued to her feet. She wiggled her bare toes in the cool night air.

"You haven't said two words since you got back," Suzanne said. "We've all been wondering what was going on. You didn't text, just left with Jack. Luke said you had something to take care of, but you know Luke. He doesn't know how to share anything. You should've seen Marcus. Whatever he was on edge about, he shared it with Ryan, and Owen must have peppered Luke with at least half a dozen questions."

Suzanne was holding a beer, one of the dark stouts she

loved, sitting in a deck chair on the front porch. Beside her, Karen welcomed the peace that drifted through her in a way she'd once taken for granted. The laughter of her family inside should have settled her more than it did.

Suzanne reached out with her sneakered foot and tapped Karen's bare toes. "Come on, earth to Karen! What's going on with you? You've been unusually quiet, so I know something is wrong—or right? I need details. Where'd you go with that man I still haven't met, and where is he now, anyway?"

Karen swirled her glass of wine and took in her practical Honda parked out front. "I was really shitty to Mom, growing up." She leaned back, looking over to her sister, who frowned and glanced back to the house.

"I'm sure she's forgiven you. We were all far from easy. But hey, look at us now." Suzanne gestured with her beer. "Come on. You're holding out on me. Where is Jack? What's going on? We all want to know."

"I loved Jack so deeply," Karen said. "I didn't tell you that part. For years, it killed me after he walked out. I never thought I would love anyone again after him, you know. And I never understood why he did it…"

Suzanne was leaning in. Karen knew she was being cryptic. "But you do now?"

She lifted her glass of wine, thinking of his family, when she heard the screen door squeak. It was Luke, beer in hand, his hair pulled back in a shaggy look. He'd gone a few days without shaving.

"Hey, Suzanne, Mom needs you in the kitchen," he said.

Suzanne frowned, looking back at him. "What for?"

Luke gestured with his beer. "I have no idea. She just asked me to send you in to help her and Jenny."

Karen knew her sister was about the last person her

mom would've asked for help in the kitchen, but Suzanne didn't argue, just stood and strode to the door.

She looked back and gestured to the chair. "That's my spot and my chair, Luke. Don't get comfortable," she said. Then she pulled the screen open and walked in, and Luke eased himself into the chair, leaning forward, looking out to the street and then over to Karen. She knew he saw more than anyone.

"Did Mom really ask you to send Suzanne in?"

A smile touched the corners of his lips, and he shook his head. "No. I told Mom I needed some one-on-one with you. She got it. She'll busy our little sister for a bit. About your call, you okay?" He patted her knee, and she shut her eyes for a second before taking another swallow of the wine, knowing she still needed to eat something.

She nodded and felt the tightness in her chest again. "I am now. Sorry. I didn't know what to do, Luke. Calling you seemed like the wisest choice, the safest for everyone."

Luke lifted his beer and took a swallow, staring straight out into the street. The evening had settled around them. "That's one fucked-up family, Karen," he said. She winced when he nudged her arm. "I checked into that story. The aunt, her name was Helda Curtis. She ran off with a handyman who was doing odd jobs around the house for the family. They moved to New Jersey, were married. She was eight months pregnant when they were both murdered in their sleep, or so the official narrative goes. The unofficial is that they were found side by side in their bed after Helda turned state's evidence against the family on charges of racketeering, trafficking, drugs, you name it. The baby cut out of her was never found, but the funny thing is that this happened the same day Jack was born, August 29." Her brother was staring at her, unsmiling.

She wondered if she'd heard him right, and she sat

back, pulling in a breath. She downed the rest of her wine before she said, "Are you sure? Luke, no…"

"Karen, some fucked-up shit goes on out there. A lot of it is above my pay grade, but yeah, I'm sure about this. I called in a favor on the team and used some unofficial back channels. Tell me what you want to do."

"I just need to sit here a second."

"As long as you want." Her brother was patient, quiet.

"Do you think Jack knows?"

Luke let out a sigh and pulled his hand over his whiskers. "I doubt it. He wouldn't have a clue. I can tell you, though, that was your warning. It's kind of how they do it. First they warn you off, then they teach you a lesson, then you're dead."

Her glass was now empty. She spotted a Lincoln SUV that she knew had to belong to Jack pulling up and parking behind her Honda. "Hey, Luke, don't tell anyone," she said.

He made a face. "This is me you're talking to, Karen," he said. "But one more thing. Your boy there didn't get his ass handed to him just because of the senator's case. Something else he was working on was what landed him on the wrong side of his family."

She knew she was frowning. Jack was still in his SUV, and she lifted her hand in a wave before turning back to Luke. "You'd better tell me."

He nodded. "He has an uncle, the CEO of a major corporation, who wanted to use a food additive he couldn't get past the FDA. So the guy made one call and was appointed the new head of the agency. Once there, he quickly approved the product, which would never have been approved otherwise. He resigned two days later and went back to his company. The profits were enormous. Your guy there got wind of it."

Her jaw slackened. "I'm going to need more wine."

Luke reached for her glass and stood. Jack was walking toward them, his suit jacket long gone and his white dress shirt sleeves rolled up.

"Luke," he said with a nod to her brother.

"Jack, can I get you a beer or something stronger?" Luke said. "I'm making a run to the store for more wine."

Jack rested his foot on the bottom step, letting his gaze linger on her. "A beer is fine," he said, and Luke was gone. Jack strode up, stood right in front of her, and then sat beside her with a groan. He rested his hand over hers, squeezing. "You sure you're okay?" He let his gaze linger.

She knew she could never tell him what his dad had said to her. "I am now that I'm back home. So what now, Jack?"

The screen door squeaked, and Luke handed Jack a beer.

"Thank you," Jack said, though Luke was already striding, keys in hand, to his older-model pickup. He climbed in, and the rumble of the truck was welcome. "I guess Missoula is off the table?"

She let out a sigh and shook her head. "I can't go back there, Jack. This is my home. My family is here, my law practice. I don't want all that stuff. This is all I want." She gestured to her brother's place, hearing the laughter of her family inside.

"I figured you would say that. I guess I'll be hanging my shingle up with yours." He lifted the beer she knew he didn't care for and took a swallow, and she realized he was serious.

"What about your family, Jack? They won't be okay with this."

He shrugged. "My mom called me while I was driving. You didn't get to meet her, and I'm sorry for that. She asked me if you made me happy. I told her like no one can. She told me to follow my heart, and she'll make sure we're left alone."

She wondered if he was that naive or if this was a lie for her benefit. "You really believe your mom can make your father, your family, leave us be?"

He let out another sigh, one she didn't know what to make of. "What they're afraid of is their secrets getting out. Yes, they'll leave us be. So how does this work with your family?" He took another swallow of beer and held it up, making a face. "This is awful…"

"I think there's more than you're telling me, but I'll let you keep your secrets. So you're ready to meet my family?" She stood up, barefoot, and held out her hand.

Jack hesitated only a second before he settled his in hers and stood too. "I guess it's now or never," he said. He slipped his arm around her, pulling her to him. "I really do love you, Karen." He leaned in and pressed a kiss to her lips.

She slid her hand over his cheek, feeling the smoothness. "I really love you too, Jack. Now time for you to meet the rest of the family."

She pulled open the screen door, Jack right behind her. Suzanne had dumped water over Owen's head, and there was laughter, then her mom yelling at them to take it outside.

This was the family she'd taken for granted, but she was grateful to have them.

Eighteen

"SO YOU'RE REALLY PACKING up, closing shop, and moving here to be with my sister?" Luke said.

Jack heard voices from out back, laughter from Karen's family. The O'Connells were the kind of family he wasn't familiar with, and he had a hard time understanding the teasing and simple fun they had together. Jack lingered in the living room of Ryan's house, taking in photos on the wall of people he didn't know.

"Karen wants to stay here in Livingston, so I'll fit what I can in her tiny condo, hang my shingle with hers in that office above the bar, and make it work. This is what Karen wants, so I'm doing it for her." Jack wasn't sure what to make of the way Luke was watching him. He wondered if he should be worried. "Karen said you're with the special forces."

Luke was buff and casual, his dark shoulder-length hair tied back in a ponytail. Something about him reminded Jack of some of his family's friends and business associates, the kind they called to handle problems no one else could. He suspected Luke understood the world he'd grown up in.

"Yup, I'm a team man," Luke said. "But I also know how this world works, and I can't figure out how you're just walking away as you say. You want to move on down and start a life away from the clutches of your family? So what gives, Jack? How about the real story?"

Jack heard laughter from the kitchen. Luke had taken another step closer to him. He realized this was the one person he couldn't bullshit. "You obviously know the kind of people I come from, the kind who run things behind the scenes."

Luke nodded. "Again, what's the real fucking story, Jack? Because I listened to you and my sister, your news about how you're going to become Curtis and O'Connell, represent the downtrodden of Montana in our little county… It doesn't work that way. What did you sell—your soul, your future, what? There was something."

"You know, I never learned how to play their game," Jack said. "I don't want to know it, to be part of it, to be one more puppet, following orders. I hear at Yale, they teach you about true leadership in the circles I was supposed to be part of. You know what qualities they prize in their puppets?"

Luke didn't pull his gaze. Jack realized all the siblings had the same vivid blue O'Connell eyes. They were such a close family. "Charisma and charm?" Luke said. "Not sure where this is going, Jack."

"I'm talking about true leadership qualities. Invariably, these people are predators. They end up behind the scenes, pushing agendas, doing as they're told. I won't ever be that. I'm not made for it. But I'm well aware that my being so vocal about their shenanigans has put a target on me and ultimately on Karen. She has the ability to compartmentalize and push on. Theater and drama are not something she thrives on, yet that's what makes up the world of my father, my family.

"I mean, how many times have you watched the news and heard someone's credibility destroyed by a few perfectly placed words? Gaslighting is a game to them. They know how to plant a story, a seed of doubt in the minds of the people, and get them to believe what they need them to. I see what they're doing, and I'll never be part of it."

Luke glanced over his shoulder, his arms crossed. "So you have a conscience? That's a good thing if you want to be with my sister, but you still haven't answered me, and you're going to need to. You've dragged Karen into this unwittingly. So what did you agree to? Are you going to run for DA, attorney general, senator, or something else?"

There it was, the question he never wanted his wife to know the answer to. Those were the final words he'd said to his father, who'd called him right after his mother had.

"I've agreed to take over the company in five years," he said. His family's public front was in textiles manufacturing, but that was only the public face of it. The reality was anything but.

"So you've bought yourself five years, and then what?" Luke said.

Jack pulled his arms across his chest. "Let's have this conversation again then. I mean, I know you work for the kinds of men who do business with my family. You follow their orders and carry out their agendas."

Luke made a face and glanced away. "So you're hoping for a miracle."

"No," Jack said. "I've got five years to become smarter than them, to make a plan, to bring them down."

Luke just grunted.

Jack heard voices and spotted Karen coming his way.

"Let's hope for my sister's sake that you're right, because a bullet in the back of your head or hers wouldn't sit well with me," Luke said. He patted Jack's shoulder. "You had better come up with plan B, and C, and D."

"What's this plan about?" Karen was barefoot, her expression questioning. She was beautiful, gorgeous, brilliant, the kind of woman a man could never manipulate.

"Just getting to know each other, is all," Jack said. "But we do need to talk plans for our office. Are you ready to go home?" He felt the weight of everything for a moment as he looked down at his wife, whom he loved so deeply, pulling her close.

"You sure it's nothing else?" she said. "I know Luke, and…"

"You know how lucky you are to have family like this, brothers who are there for you?" Jack said. "Luke's just helping me figure some things out. He's a good man."

Karen pulled back, made a face, and glanced to her brother and then back to Jack. "He is, but you forget, Jack, this is your family now, too." Then she rose on her tiptoes and offered a kiss, which he took, pulling her closer and hugging her. When he looked up over her head, he spotted Luke watching, a brother who had her back and who understood clearly the tightrope Jack walked.

His world was bigger. The people his father knew were watching him, and nothing was as simple as everyone thought.

It wasn't black and white, or shades of gray. It was all of the above. But today was today, and five years was a long way away. Right now, all he needed to worry about was staying under the radar and making sure his wife was happy.

Turn the page for a sneak peek of
THE QUIET DAY the next book in *THE O'CONNELLS*
Available in print, eBook & audio

The Quiet Day

As a female firefighter in a small town, Suzanne O'Connell finds herself trapped in a dangerous situation with two men. And when the stakes turn deadly, trusting the wrong man could put her life in jeopardy.

As a female firefighter in a small town, Suzanne O'Connell knows that every day will go one of two ways: Either nothing happens, or she suddenly finds herself in over her head. Firefighters never, ever say the words "It's a quiet day!"—because that's when all hell breaks loose, and their peaceful, easy day suddenly turns into their worst nightmare. This is exactly what happens to Suzanne when she finds herself trapped with Harold Waters, local law enforcement officer and her old flame, and fellow fireman Toby Chandler, who, according to everyone, is the kind of guy you want watching your back.

In an unusual turn of events, the stakes turn deadly, and

Suzanne discovers that trusting the wrong man could leave her life hanging in the balance.

The Quiet Day

CHAPTER 1

"YOU GOING to eat that entire tub of ice cream, or do the rest of us get to have some?" Marcus said as he strode into his kitchen, where Suzanne was sitting alone after rummaging through his freezer for the ice cream she'd brought over. She just stared at him as she jabbed a large tablespoon into the big tub of strawberry swirl again and lifted out a big hunk.

"Help yourself," she said around the mouthful, feeling the brain freeze the minute she swallowed.

Marcus shook his head, taking the tub of ice cream from her and moving it near the sink, away from her. He reached for three bowls from the cupboard, and Suzanne leaned against the nicked-up blue and white counter. Marcus and Charlotte's house was small, dated. The kitchen was closed off from the rest of the house, and the old wood floor squeaked in places, but it had a big yard and was close to their mom's place, and Eva had her own bedroom.

Suzanne could hear the voices of her family coming

from the small living room as she took another bite from the hunk of ice cream still on her spoon.

"So why are you hiding out in here?" Marcus said with only a glance over his shoulder. He was in a faded army green T-shirt and blue jeans, sock-footed, and his dark wavy hair appeared freshly cut. He also seemed very much at home, the family man with an instant family, a role she hadn't expected for him. Six-year-old Eva came running into the kitchen in a red and white flowered T-shirt and pajama pants and wrapped her arms around his leg, standing on his foot.

"Can I have ice cream, please…?" she said. She was so damn sweet and tiny.

Marcus smiled down at her and rustled her shoulder-length brown hair, also freshly cut. Suzanne recalled that her mom had booked a "granddaughters hair day" for Eva and Alison only the day before at Delilah's Hair, a friend's salon.

"Just dishing yours up now, sweet pea," Marcus said as he lifted her and sat her on the counter. Suzanne loved the nickname he had given her. "Here, you can help," he continued and gave Eva the scoop, his hand over hers.

Suzanne finished off the ice cream on her spoon, holding it up. Her cell phone was silent, its screen still black, and she double checked to see if the thing was powered on.

"You didn't answer me, Suzanne. What's going on?" Marcus asked as he helped Eva down and handed her a bowl. She walked with it back into the living room, all smiles.

"You sure are good with her," Suzanne said, then gestured toward him with her spoon. "You given any thought to what will happen when her mom is released from prison?"

Marcus was still dishing ice cream into three other bowls, and he let out a sigh before shaking his head. "You're changing the subject—and that's a long ways off, not something I'm worrying about right now or putting on the table for discussion. So what's up with you? Because you're off tonight. How come, problems?" He gestured with the empty scoop to her and the cell phone she was holding, and she forced herself to put it down on the counter.

She shook her head. "No, everything's fine," she said, not sure what to make of his face and the way he was looking at her.

"Bullshit, Suzanne. You're usually way better at hiding your off-ness, so what's got you so glued to that phone? You've been texting someone, and all I can figure is whoever it is has you kind of distracted. You've barely said anything to anyone, just glanced at your phone every thirty seconds. This isn't like you. Then you slipped off alone to the kitchen, eating away your stress, as Charlotte says."

She hadn't realized he'd been watching. She had to fight the urge to pick up her phone, to look again at the texts that had gone unanswered.

"The silent treatment?" Marcus let out a sarcastic laugh.

"It's nothing, really," Suzanne said. "And I wasn't stress eating," she added for effect.

He turned around, tossed the scoop in the sink, and wiped his hands on a dishtowel before gesturing to the ice cream lid, which was still beside her on the counter. "Whatever you say, Suzanne."

She reached for it and crossed the kitchen to hand it to him, just shaking her head when he gestured as if asking whether she wanted more. He had a way of making her seem defensive when she was anything but.

"Just for the record, Suzanne, you can keep telling me it's nothing, but I know it isn't, or you wouldn't be so distracted. You may as well just save us all the aggravation and tell me." He was still leaning on the counter and didn't look as if he were leaving anytime soon.

"Fine, you want to know? It's just someone who hasn't answered me, is all. We kind of had plans, and then…" She shrugged.

His expression darkened. "Please tell me we're not talking about that asshole, Toby."

There it was, exactly why she hadn't wanted to say anything.

"Tell me how you really feel, Marcus." She was still holding the empty spoon and thought of the tub of ice cream she'd been drowning her sorrows in moments earlier. Yup, she could definitely have used another scoop —but it wasn't stress eating, because she didn't do that.

"Well, I'll take that as my answer," he said in a tone that bothered her. "What the hell are you doing, Suzanne? You can do so much better. He's got nothing going for him. He doesn't have a sincere bone in his body, and that phony plastic smile he gives to everyone…shallow, no depth at all. If I really have to dig to find something redeeming about the guy, that should tell you something. I mean, why him? I don't understand why you'd do that to yourself."

She had to fight the urge to roll her shoulders as he went on. At the same time, she wasn't too inclined to share anything about her reasoning. The chemistry she had with Toby didn't happen with just any guy.

"You're being overdramatic, Marcus. Toby is a good guy."

Marcus just shook his head, and the look he tossed her said he didn't agree. She knew there was no love lost there, though the dislike was one sided. Her brother had never made any excuses for how he felt about Toby, but Toby had never said the same about him.

"Really? How about the fact that he's also your boss now, even though you trained him? Doesn't that get to you even just a little bit, Suzanne? Because it should." Marcus lifted the bowls of ice cream, already jabbed with spoons, and stepped over to her.

She had to remind herself that Marcus knew which of her emotional buttons to push. She pulled in a breath and forced herself to look away, then back to him. "That wasn't on Toby. You should know that. Can I blame him for wanting the lieutenant job?" She shrugged, trying to put some lightness in her tone.

She didn't want to admit that she still felt as if the rug had been yanked out from under her, considering she'd expected the promotion and had deserved it, yet when it happened, she realized she hadn't even been considered. She pulled in another breath and took in the way Marcus was still watching her as if waiting for her reaction.

"Yeah, you can, Suzanne, and you should. He didn't earn it, and he doesn't appreciate you. You dating him?"

There it was, the million-dollar question of just how committed Toby was to her. What could she say?

"It's not that serious, you know—and how is this any of your business, anyway?"

Marcus took another step toward her, but before he could reply, Charlotte stepped into the kitchen.

"Hey," she said. "Was wondering what was taking you so long. Alison is asking for her ice cream, since Eva is already done. Did I walk in on something?" Her long dark hair was hanging loose. Suzanne swore she could make anything look stunning, including the faded jeans and old T-shirt of Marcus's that she wore now. Some women just had that amazing, sexy, curvy appeal, but Suzanne never had.

She watched as Charlotte slid her hand around Marcus's waist, and he handed one of the bowls to her. Suzanne hoped her envy didn't show. He pressed a kiss to Charlotte's lips—and, damn, their closeness was uncomfortable. She wished they wouldn't do that right when they were having a conversation.

"No, nothing, just Suzanne mooning over Toby," Marcus said. "Let me guess: You've texted or called, and he hasn't called you back?" The way he was including Charlotte in this private conversation only added salt to her wound.

Here she was, lonely on a Saturday night when she'd wanted—no, expected to be out with Toby. They had plans, she assumed, but maybe not. She was now questioning what they had actually agreed on. Was she misreading things? She hated feeling like she was assuming something in whatever this was between them.

Charlotte seemed to hesitate as she gave everything to Suzanne, who now felt as if her personal life had taken center stage, out in the open for everyone to scrutinize. That was something she didn't want.

"I texted. He must be busy," she said. Even as it fell from her lips, she knew it sounded pathetic. It was unlike her to make excuses for anyone. Her brother only grunted, and Charlotte winced.

"He's blowing you off," Marcus said. "More than likely, he's with someone else. You ever thought of that?"

Then her cell phone dinged, and she practically landed on it, seeing a text from Toby.

Sorry, babe. Got hung up. How about my place in an hour?

She held the phone in front of her, feeling excitement or something. When Marcus rested his hand over the phone, she thought he was going to take it from her. As she lifted her gaze to her brother's, his expression was anything but friendly.

"Please do not be one of those girls," he said. Then he stepped away, inclining his head and glancing toward Charlotte and the bowl of ice cream she was holding before walking out of the kitchen. She could hear him calling Alison.

Charlotte gave everything to Suzanne. "Don't mind Marcus. He just loves you, is all, and doesn't want to see some guy messing with you, considering how he feels about Toby."

Of course, she didn't want to hear that, especially from Charlotte. Maybe that was why she felt so on edge as she pulled in another breath, realizing she was still gripping her spoon.

"Thanks, but Marcus is just sticking his nose where it doesn't belong, and he's way off base with Toby. Anyway, as I said, it's not serious. It's just a thing." She shrugged, feeling the bitterness in the way the words rolled off her tongue. She couldn't put a label on this thing happening between her and Toby. Yeah, she really liked him, but it seemed the effort was entirely on her side.

Charlotte must have known, as she just offered a smile and lifted her hands in a gesture Suzanne hoped meant she'd leave it alone and not offer an opinion. "You know, I'm not too sure about Marcus being off base, Suzanne. One thing I know about your brother is how well he reads everyone, better than most—and Toby, he's a player. Just watch yourself, because from where I'm sitting, I can see that Toby is possibly stringing you along. When he texts you and tells you to come running, you may want to ask him who he was with before you."

Before Suzanne could set her straight, Charlotte rested

her hand on her arm and walked out of the kitchen. Then her phone dinged.

Let me know if you're coming, Toby wrote, and he added two flirty emojis that would've been cute if she hadn't just had Charlotte and Marcus insinuate that Toby wasn't being straight with her.

The problem was that they just didn't know him.

As she dumped her spoon into the sink, still holding her phone, she saw the three dots that meant he was sending another text, but she was reminded of Charlotte's words. Where had he been, and what had happened to their plan of grabbing a few beers, going out together? Now, he was two hours late.

About the Author

"Lorhainne Eckhart is one of my go to authors when I want a guaranteed good book. So many twists and turns, but also so much love and such a strong sense of family."

(LORA W., REVIEWER)

New York Times & USA Today bestseller Lorhainne Eckhart writes Raw Relatable Real Romance is best known for her big family romances series, where "Morals and family are running themes. Danger, romance, and a drive to do what is right will see you glued to the page." As one fan calls her, she is the "Queen of the family saga." (aherman) writing "the ups and downs of what goes on within a family but also with some suspense, angst and of course a bit of romance thrown in for good measure." Follow Lorhainne on Bookbub to receive alerts on New Releases and Sales and join her mailing list at LorhainneEckhart.com for her Monday Blog, books news, giveaways and FREE reads. With over 120 books, audiobooks, and multiple series published and available at all retailers now translated into six languages. She is a multiple recipient of the Readers' Favorite Award for Suspense and Romance, and lives in the Pacific Northwest on an island, is the mother of three, her oldest has autism and she is an advocate for never giving up on your dreams.

"Lorhainne Eckhart has this uncanny way of just hitting the spot every time with her books."

(CAROLINE L., REVIEWER)

The O'Connells: *The O'Connells of Livingston, Montana are not your typical family. A riveting collection of stories surrounding the ups and downs of what goes on within a family but also with some suspense, angst and of course a bit of romance thrown in for good measure "I thought I loved the Friessens, but I absolutely adore the O'Connell's. Each and every book has totally different genres of stories but the one thing in common is how she is able to wrap it around the family which is the heart of each story." (C. Logue)*

The Friessens: *An emotional big family romance series, the Friessen family siblings find their relationships tested, lay their hearts on the line, and discover lasting love! "Lorhainne Eckhart is one of my go to authors when I want a guaranteed good book. So many twists and turns, but also so much love and such a strong sense of family." (Lora W., Reviewer)*

The Parker Sisters: *The Parker Sisters are a close-knit family, and like any other family they have their ups and downs. "Eckhart has crafted another intense family drama…The character development is outstanding, and the emotional investment is high…" (Aherman, Reviewer)*

The McCabe Brothers: *Join the five McCabe siblings on their journeys to the dark and dangerous side of love! An intense, exhilarating collection of romantic thrillers you won't want to miss. — "Eckhart has a new series that is definitely worth the read. The queen of the family saga started this series with a spin-off of her wildly successful Friessen series." From a Readers' Favorite award—winning author and "queen of the family saga" (Aherman)*

Billy Jo McCabe Mystery: *The social worker and the cop, an unlikely couple drawn together on a small, secluded Pacific Northwest island where nothing is as it seems. Protecting the innocent comes at a cost, and what seems to be a sleepy, quiet town is anything but.*

Lorhainne loves to hear from her readers! You can connect with me at:
www.LorhainneEckhart.com
lorhainneeckhart.le@gmail.com

Also by Lorhainne Eckhart

The Outsider Series
The Forgotten Child (Brad and Emily)
A Baby and a Wedding *(An Outsider Series Short)*
Fallen Hero (Andy, Jed, and Diana)
The Awakening (Andy and Laura)
Secrets (Jed and Diana)
Runaway (Andy and Laura)
Overdue *(An Outsider Series Short)*
The Unexpected Storm (Neil and Candy)
The Wedding (Neil and Candy)

The Friessens: A New Beginning
The Deadline (Andy and Laura)
The Price to Love (Neil and Candy)
A Different Kind of Love (Brad and Emily)
A Vow of Love, A Friessen Family Christmas

The Friessens
The Reunion
The Bloodline (Andy & Laura)
The Promise (Diana & Jed)
The Business Plan (Neil & Candy)
The Decision (Brad & Emily)
First Love (Katy)
Family First
Leave the Light On
In the Moment
In the Family

In the Silence
In the Charm
Unexpected Consequences
It Was Always You
The First Time I Saw You
Welcome to My Arms
Welcome to Boston
I'll Always Love You
Ground Rules
A Reason to Breathe
You Are My Everything
Anything For You
The Homecoming
Stay Away From My Daughter
The Bad Boy
A Place of Our Own
The Visitor
All About Devon
Long Past Dawn
How to Heal a Heart
Keep Me in Your Heart

The O'Connells
The Neighbor
The Third Call
The Secret Husband
The Quiet Day
The Commitment
The Missing Father
The Hometown Hero
Justice
The Family Secret
The Fallen O'Connell

The Return of the O'Connells
And The She Was Gone
The Stalker
The O'Connell Family Christmas
The Girl Next Door
Broken Promises
The Gatekeeper
The Hunted

The McCabe Brothers
Don't Stop Me (Vic)
Don't Catch Me (Chase)
Don't Run From Me (Aaron)
Don't Hide From Me (Luc)
Don't Leave Me (Claudia)
Out of Time

A Billy Jo McCabe Mystery
Nothing As it Seems
Hiding in Plain Sight
The Cold Case
The Trap
Above the Law
The Stranger at the Door
The Children
The Last Stand
The Charity
The Sacrifice

The Wilde Brothers
The One
The Honeymoon, A Wilde Brothers Short
Friendly Fire

Not Quite Married, A Wilde Brothers Short
A Matter of Trust
The Reckoning, A Wilde Brothers Christmas
Traded
Unforgiven
The Holiday Bride

Married in Montana
His Promise
Love's Promise
A Promise of Forever

The Parker Sisters
Thrill of the Chase
The Dating Game
Play Hard to Get
What We Can't Have
Go Your Own Way
A June Wedding

Kate & Walker
One Night
Edge of Night
Last Night

Walk the Right Road Series
The Choice
Lost and Found
Merkaba
Bounty
Blown Away: The Final Chapter
He Came Back

The Saved Series

Saved
Vanished
Captured

Single Titles
Loving Christine